# KING SOLOMON'S
# MINES

# KING SOLOMON'S MINES

Sir Henry Rider Haggard

An imprint of Om Books International

Reprinted in 2020

Om KIDZ | Om Books International

**Corporate & Editorial Office**
A-12, Sector 64, Noida 201 301
Uttar Pradesh, India
Phone: +91 120 477 4100
Email: editorial@ombooks.com
Website: www.ombooksinternational.com

**Sales Office**
107, Ansari Road, Darya Ganj
New Delhi 110 002, India
Phone: +91 11 4000 9000
Email: sales@ombooks.com
Website: www.ombooks.com



ISBN: 978-93-85031-45-8

Printed in India

10 9 8 7 6 5 4 3

# Contents

| | | |
|---|---|---|
| 1. | I Meet Sir Henry Curtis | 7 |
| 2. | The Legend of Solomon's Mines | 21 |
| 3. | Umbopa Enters Our Service | 37 |
| 4. | An Elephant Hunt | 43 |
| 5. | Our March | 53 |
| 6. | Water! Water! | 63 |
| 7. | Solomon's Road | 71 |
| 8. | We Enter Kukuanaland | 89 |
| 9. | Twala the King | 97 |
| 10. | The Witch Hunt | 109 |
| 11. | We Give a Sign | 121 |
| 12. | Before the Battle | 135 |
| 13. | The Attack | 145 |
| 14. | The Last Stand of the Greys | 153 |
| 15. | Good Falls Sick | 165 |
| 16. | The Place of Death | 175 |
| 17. | Solomon's Treasure Chamber | 185 |
| 18. | We Abandon Hope | 197 |
| 19. | Ignosi's Farewell | 209 |
| 20. | Found | 223 |
| | About the Author | 234 |
| | Characters | 235 |
| | Questions | 237 |

## Chapter One

# I Meet Sir Henry Curtis

It is a curious thing that at the age of fifty-five, I am taking up a pen to try to write history. I am writing about the events that helped me make a fortune. But, I do not think I would go through the ordeal of the last fifteen or sixteen months again for it.

To start with, let me try to list down my reasons for writing this book.

First, because Sir Henry Curtis and Captain John Good asked me to. Second, because I am held back at Durban due to the pain in my left leg. I have been having this recurrent pain ever since that detestable lion planted his sharp teeth on my leg.

Third, because I want my son, Harry, to be entertained by our adventure. He is studying in London to become a doctor and reading this book will keep him out of mischief for a week or so at the very least.

The fourth and last reason is because I have a strange story to tell. The story is strange for many reasons. Among them, one is that it has no women in it except for Foulata and that Gagool. That is, if you consider her to be a woman.

Well, I'd better begin my story...

I am Allan Quatermain, a travelling trader and a hunter. I have been involved in numerous fights and killed many men during my time. But, I would like to clarify this; I have shed blood only in self-defence.

I was born a gentleman. But have I remained one? I don't quite know. I have had a lot to do with slaves.

I think I will scratch out the word "slaves" for I do not like it.

As for being gentlemen, I have known natives who are and I have also known mean people with lots of money and fresh out from home, too, who are not.

My adventure began eighteen months ago when I had been elephant hunting beyond Bamangwato. Everything went wrong with that trip. I met with bad luck, got the fever badly, got overcharged at a hotel and I was finally determined to go back to Natal. I bought a berth on the steamer called Dunkeld and went aboard. In the afternoon, we were joined by passengers from Edinburgh Castle that sailed in from England. Soon, Dunkeld was at sea.

Among the passengers were two gentlemen who aroused my curiosity. One was a tall, fine-looking gentleman of about thirty. He had yellow hair, a thick yellow beard, clear-cut features and large, grey eyes. He seemed to remind me of someone, but I could not remember who.

His companion was a broad man of medium height. He was stout and dark, and wore an eye-glass in his right eye.

The eye-glass seemed to reside in there, for it had no string. Afterwards, I found out that he took off his eye glass when he went to sleep, along with his false teeth, of which he had two sets.

I judged him to be a naval officer and I was proved right. He was Captain James Good, a lieutenant. He must have been thirty-one years old. He had been turned out of Her Majesty's employment after seventeen years of service. This is what people who serve the Queen have to expect: to be shot out into the cold world to find a living just when they are beginning to really understand their work.

It was evening. I was standing by the engines, watching the pendulum's movement, when I heard someone behind me say, "That pendulum is wrong."

I turned around and saw Captain Good.

"What makes you think so?" I asked him, dreading that I might have to listen to an officer of the Royal Navy when he gets on to that particular subject.

But before he could answer my question, the dinner bell rang and I accompanied the captain to his table.

Sir Henry Curtis was already seated by the table when we reached there.

Captain Good sat next to him and I sat opposite them. The captain asked a lot of questions. Soon, the talk veered to elephants. Someone sitting at the table commented, "Sir, you've found the right man to learn about elephants. Hunter Quatermain should be able to tell you about elephants if anybody can."

Sir Henry, who had been sitting quietly until now, suddenly looked at me curiously. "Excuse me, sir," he said in a low deep voice. "But is your name Allan Quatermain?"

I said that it was.

The big man made no further remark, but I heard him mutter "fortunate" into his beard. Sir Henry remained quiet throughout dinner after that. But when I got up to take my leave, he asked me to join them in his cabin to smoke a pipe.

The cabin was spacious. We sat down on comfortable chairs and lit our pipes.

"Mr Quatermain," said Sir Henry Curtis. "Two years ago, I believe you were at a place called Bamangwato, to the north of the Transvaal."

I was rather surprised to hear that he was aware of my movements. "I was," I said.

"You were trading there, were you not?" asked Captain Good.

"I was. I took up a wagon-load of goods and camped outside the settlement till I sold them."

Sir Henry had a curious look in his eye. He asked, "Did you happen to meet a man called Neville there?"

"Yes. He stayed with me for a fortnight to rest his oxen before heading to the interior. He left at the beginning of May in a wagon with a hunter called Jim. He planned to trek as far as Inyati, where he would sell his wagon and go further on foot. In fact, a few months back I got a letter from a lawyer asking me if I knew what had happened to him. I replied in the best way I could."

"Yes," said Sir Henry, "your letter was forwarded to me."

I was surprised to hear this. Sir Henry continued, "Do you know or can you guess the reasons of my — of Mr Neville's journey to the northward? Do you happen to know where he was going?"

"I heard something," I said and stopped. The subject was one that I didn't care to discuss.

Sir Henry and Captain Good looked at each other. Captain Good nodded.

"Mr Quatermain," continued Sir Henry, "I am going to tell you a story and I ask your advice, and perhaps your assistance. The agent who forwarded me your letter told me that you are greatly respected and can be trusted completely."

I was embarrassed.

"Mr Neville was my brother."

"Oh," I said, startled. I now knew whom Sir Henry reminded me of when I first saw him.

"He was my one and only brother. He was called George. Until five years ago, we were never apart from each other for more than a month. However, my father died without leaving a will. As per the law of England, I inherited everything. George, my brother, was left penniless. We fought bitterly. In my anger, I behaved unjustly towards my brother," said Sir Henry.

Here, Captain Good looked solemn and nodded his head vigorously in agreement.

Sir Henry continued, "Later, I found out that my brother George withdrew the few hundred pounds that he had in his bank account. He took up the name of Neville and came to Africa, hoping to make his fortune. Three years passed by and I heard nothing of my brother, though I wrote to him several times. I have no doubt that the letters never reached him. I was worried about him. I then started sending enquiries concerning my brother. Mr Quatermain, your letter was the only ray of hope.

So, to cut a long story short," said Sir Henry, "I made up my mind to come out and look for him myself, and Captain Good was so kind as to come with me."

"Nothing better to do," explained Captain Good, smiling politely.

"But tell me, what was it that you heard about my brother's journey at Bamangwato?" Sir Henry asked me.

"What I heard has stayed with me. I have never mentioned it to anyone until today," I answered.

"I heard that he was going to look for Solomon's Mines."

## Chapter Two

# The Legend of Solomon's Mines

Sir Henry and the captain, who had travelled around the world twice, had never heard of Solomon's Mines.

I agreed to tell them, if they promised not to tell another soul. They agreed.

"Well," I began, "elephant hunters only bother to know about the facts of life and the ways of the natives. However, thirty years ago, I met a man called Evans and learnt about something very different. He told me about Solomon's Mines. It was a full moon night and we were roasting meat over the fire when Evans began his tale."

Evans said, "I know a place where a treasure is buried. Do you know the Suliman Mountains to the north-west of Mushakulumbwe?" I told him I didn't.

"Ah," he said, "that is where Suliman really had his mines, his diamond mines."

I realised that 'Suliman' is but a corruption of Solomon. I remembered an old witch doctor in Manica telling me that the people who lived on those mountains were a branch of the Zulus, but they were finer and bigger. She had said that great wizards lived among them, people who knew the secret of a mine with bright stones.

I found Evan's story amusing and interesting. The next morning, I bid farewell. Poor Evans died the next year. For twenty years, I did not think of the matter.

Twenty years later, I heard something more definite about Suliman's Mountains. I was at Sitanda's Kraal, a place devoid of food. I developed a fever and set up a tent to recover. One day, a tall and thin Portuguese with dark

eyes and a curling grey moustache called Jose Silvestre came with his servant. We conversed in English and Portuguese. While leaving the next day, he said, "If we ever meet again I shall be the richest man in the world."

I found this amusing. I watched him venture out for the great desert, wondering if he was mad or what he thought he was going to find. A week later, I recovered and forgot all about Jose.

Then, one evening, while watching the sunset and having my supper, I saw a figure, creeping along on its hands and knees.

At once, I sent one of my hunters to help him. It was Jose Silvestre. He was reduced to just a bag of bones and skin. His face was bright yellow with fever and his large dark eyes were protruding out of his head. He moaned, "Water! For god's sake, water!" And I saw that his lips were cracked. His tongue was swollen and blackish. I held his head and gave him water mixed with milk.

He drank it in large gulps. Soon, struck with fever, he collapsed and began to rave about

Suliman's Mountains, diamonds and the desert. I carried him inside the tent to look after him and nurse him back to health.

At dawn I woke up and saw Silvestre sitting and gazing at the desert where a ray of sunlight lit one of the tallest of the Suliman Mountains more than a hundred miles away.

"There it is!" The dying man cried in his native Portuguese. "But I shall never reach it, never. No one will ever reach it!"

"Friend," he said, turning towards me. "Are you still here? My eyes grow dark."

"Yes," I said. "Lie down and rest."

"Ay," he answered, "I shall rest soon for eternity. I am dying! You have been good to me. I will give you the writing. Maybe you will get there, if you can cross the desert which has killed my poor servant and is now killing me."

From his shirt, he removed a Boer tobacco pouch. "Untie it," he said.

I did so and extracted a bit of torn yellow linen on which something was written in rusty letters. Inside this rag was a paper.

Jose continued in a feeble voice, "This paper is the key. It took me years to read. My ancestor Jose da Silvestre was one of the first Portuguese to land on these shores 300 years ago. He wrote it when he was dying on those mountains where no white man before or after him has passed."

Jose da Silvestre's slave, who had waited for him on the foot of the mountain, had brought the writing home to Delagoa.

"The paper has been in the family ever since but no one had bothered to read it until I did. And I have lost my life over it. But another may succeed and become the richest man in the world. Only, give it to no one, senor; go yourself!" advised the Portuguese man. An hour later, he was dead.

"God rest him!" I said as I buried him.

Listening to my tale, a curious captain and Sir Henry asked, "What was in the document?"

"Well, gentlemen," I told then, putting down my glass and looking at them, "I have never showed it to anybody except a drunken old

Portuguese trader who translated it for me. The original rag is at my home in Durban but I have the English version with me, with a facsimile of the map. Here it is."

*I, Jose da Silvestre, am dying of hunger in a little cave on the north side, where there is no snow on the north side of the peak of the southernmost of the two mountains that I have now named Sheba's Breasts.*

*I write this in the year 1590 with a cleft bone upon a remnant of my clothing, using my blood as ink. If my slave should find it when he comes, he should take it to Delagoa, and let my friend (name illegible) bring the matter to the knowledge of the king.*

*The king may send an army which, if they live through the desert and the mountains, and can overcome the brave Kukuanas, will make him the richest king since Solomon. With my own eyes I have seen the countless diamonds stored in Solomon's treasure chamber behind the white Death.*

*But through the treachery of Gagool, the witchfinder, I could barely come here alive.*

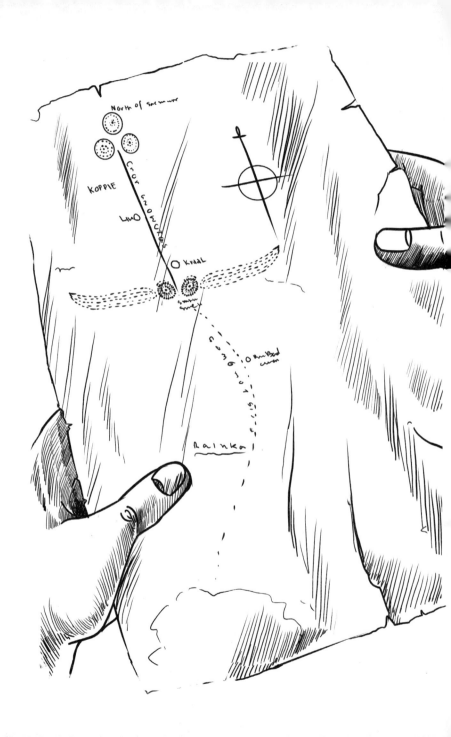

*Let him, who comes, follow the map and climb the snow of Sheba's left breast till he reaches the peak, on the north side of which is the great road which Solomon made. From this point further, journey for three days to reach the king's palace. Let him kill Gagool. Pray for my soul. Farewell. Jose da Silvestre.*

An astonished silence followed after I had finished reading.

"It's a strange tale that you tell us, Mr Quatermain," said Sir Henry. "I hope you are not making it up."

"You shall see the original map and writing when we reach Durban," I answered solemnly.

"Now," I went on, "about your brother. I knew the man, Jim, who was with him. Jim was a good hunter and extremely clever. I had asked him, "Jim, where are you off to? Is it elephants?"

"No, Baas," he answered, "we are going after something that is worth much more than ivory and gold."

"And what might that be?" I had asked curiously. Which is when Jim said, "Baas, we are going after diamonds."

"Diamonds!" I exclaimed. "Then, you should head for the Fields!"

"Baas, have you ever heard of Suliman's Berg or Solomon's Mountains?"

"I have heard a foolish story, Jim."

"It is no story, Baas."

"You and your master will serve as food for the vultures Jim, if he tries to reach Suliman's country," I told him.

Half an hour later Jim came back running.

"Goodbye, Baas," he said. "I wanted to say goodbye to you. My master is going to Suliman's Berg to make his fortune."

"Oh!" I said. "Jim, will you take a note to your master and promise not to give it to him till you reach Inyati?"

He nodded. So I took a scrap of paper and wrote the directions to Solomon's Road on it. "Now, Jim," I said, "when you give this to your master, tell him he had better follow the advice on it implicitly."

He took the note and ran to the wagon.

That was, Sir Henry, the last time I saw them,"
I ended my story.

"Mr Quatermain," said Sir Henry, "I am
going to look for my brother. I am going to trace
him to Suliman's Mountains and over them if
necessary. I will stop only when I either find him
or I know that he is dead. Would you like to come
with me?"

"No, thank you, Sir Henry," I answered. "If
we venture, we would probably end up like poor
Silvestre. I have a son who is dependent on me,
so I cannot afford to risk my life foolishly."

Both Sir Henry and Captain Good looked
very disappointed.

"Mr Quatermain," said the former, "I am keen
to go and I will pay for all the expenses of this
journey. I can also pay you any amount that you
will ask for before we undertake this journey.
Moreover, I will make arrangements to see that
your son is well provided for, in case something
untoward happens to you.

I need you to come with us. If we are fortunate enough to reach this place and find diamonds, they shall belong to you and Good equally. I do not want them."

"Sir Henry," I said, "this is a very generous proposal. It is the biggest job that I have ever been offered. Therefore, I can only ask that you give me some time to think over it."

# Chapter Three

# Umbopa Enters Our Service

I thought about Sir Henry's offer all throughout our journey to Natal. Finally, as we steamed past the coast of Natal, my desire as a father to provide for my son made me agree.

On the last evening, I told Sir Henry, "First, all expenses shall be paid by you and if we find some valuables, they must be divided equally between me and the Captain. Second, you must pay me 500 pounds. Third, if we die, then you must pay my boy, Harry, who is studying medicine in London at Guy's Hospital, a pension of 200 pounds a year for five years. By then, he shall complete his education and be able to earn his living."

"I accept these terms gladly," said Sir Henry.

I added, "I must warn you, we may not return alive from this journey."

Sir Henry, who was very determined, said, "We must take our chances."

On the next day, we went ashore and I started making preparations for the journey.

I purchased a wagon for 125 pounds, which was twenty-two feet long. It could accommodate a bed for two and a rack for rifles along with other conveniences. I also bought a pair of oxen. Then, I bought a team of twenty Zulu oxen. Zulu oxen are small, light and survive where other cattle may not.

We stocked medicines as per Good's suggestion. Good had passed a course on medical and surgical instruction while he had served as a naval officer. For arms, we bought everything from elephant guns to shot guns to revolvers and ample cartridges.

Additionally, we hired a Zulu driver and leader, named Goza and Tom respectively.

We needed three servants. We hired two servants immediately. One was Ventvogel, a Hottentot. He was also an excellent animal tracker. The other servant was a little Zulu named Khiva who spoke English perfectly.

The third Zulu presented himself to us on the evening before we started our journey. He was thirty years old and his skin was a very light colour for a Zulu. Since I knew his language, I could easily communicate with him.

"Well," I said. "What is your name and what do you want?"

"Umbopa," answered the man in a slow, deep voice. "I have heard that you are going on a great expedition far into the North to the Solomon's mountains. Is this true?"

"Why do you want to know where we are going? Also, what is your name and where is your kraal?" I asked him doubtfully. I found him a little suspicious.

"My name is Umbopa. I am of the Zulu people, yet not of them. The house of my tribe is in the

far North. I have no kraal. I have wandered for many years.

I have been working in Natal. But I do not belong here and I would like to go back to the North again. I want no money from you, but I am a brave man and I am worth my place and meat."

I was rather puzzled. Sir Henry listened with interest as I translated Umbopa's story. He told me to ask Umbopa to stand up. Umbopa did so.

He was a fine looking native, who was about six foot three and well-proportioned. Sir Henry walked up to him and said in English, "I like your looks, Mr Umbopa. I will take you as my servant on this journey."

Umbopa evidently understood him, for he answered in Zulu, "It is well."

# Chapter Four

# An Elephant Hunt

It was a long journey of over a thousand miles from Durban to Sitanda's Kraal. Of this, we had to cross the last 300 miles by foot.

We had left Durban at the end of January and we reached Sitanda's Kraal only in the second week of May. We set up a camp there.

I will not tell you all the incidents that happened along the way, except for this one, which I think you will find interesting.

At Inyati, we had to leave our comfortable wagon and the twelve surviving oxen with Goz and Tom, our driver and leader.

Then, accompanied by Umbopa, Khiva, Ventvogel, and half a dozen bearers whom we hired on the spot, we continued on foot upon our wild quest.

After about a fortnight's march from Inyati, we came across a beautiful well-watered woodland country. Seeing the fallen trees and crushed fruit, I realised that elephants frequented this place.

One evening, after a long day's march, we came to a lovely spot. It was a dry river bed with little pools of water, trodden with the hoof-prints of game. Facing this hill was a park-like plain and all around stretched a sea of pathless, silent bushes. We set up our camp here and soon shot a game. We ate our simple meal under the moonlight and sat around smoking.

There I was, with my short grizzled hair sticking up, and Sir Henry, contrasting my look with his long yellow locks. But, perhaps the most curious looking was Captain Good. He was absolutely clean, tidy and well dressed. Even his eye-glass and false teeth appeared to be perfect.

We heard the sound of elephants. Both Captain Good and Sir Henry were keen and excited to hunt an elephant. I told them that it was not easy, but they insisted. So it was decided that we would hunt elephants the next day. After making our preparations for the hunt, we fell asleep.

We woke up at dawn and, after eating a little breakfast, we left the camp, accompanied by Umbopa, Khiva and Ventvogel. We left the other natives behind and carried our three eight-bore rifles, a good supply of ammunition, and of course, our large water-bottles with us.

We found the broad elephant trail easily. Ventvogel examined the trail and told us that it appeared to be made by a herd of twenty to thirty elephants; most of them were likely to be full-grown bulls. I knew that the herd was near, seeing the uprooted trees, bruised leaves and bark and their droppings. The herd had moved on during the night.

Though it was just 9 am, it was already very hot. We soon caught sight of the herd–it had about thirty elephants, just as Ventvogel had predicted. It was a splendid sight to see them standing in a hollow, flapping their great ears. We moved closer; now the herd was only about two hundred yards from us. We carefully inched closer and reached within forty yards of the herd.

Right in front of us stood three, massive, grown elephants. I whispered to the others that I would take the middle one; Sir Henry could take the elephant to the left and Captain Good could take the elephant with the big tusks on the right.

"Now," I whispered.

Boom! Boom! Boom! The three heavy rifles fired and down came Sir Henry's elephant, dead as a hammer, shot right through the heart. I had to fire two bullets to make my elephant fall down.

Then I turned to see how Good had fared with the big bull.

I had heard the bull screaming with rage and pain as I was shooting at my elephant. The captain explained that after he had fired the bullet, the elephant had turned and charged blindly towards our camp.

Meanwhile, the herd had panicked and fled wildly in the other direction. We debated if we should go after the wounded elephant or go after the herd.

We concluded that we should go after the herd. We chased it for two hours, finally found it and killed a few more elephants. After the natives had taken out the hearts of two elephants, we turned back towards our camp.

We were resting at a place very close to our camp when Good saw a herd of elands. He was curious about them, so, he handed his rifle to Umbopa and went towards the antelope herd with Khiva.

Sir Henry and I sat around admiring the setting sun.

We suddenly heard an elephant's scream. The next moment, we saw its huge and rushing form with uplifted trunk. In the next second, we saw Good and Khiva running back towards us. They were being chased by the wounded bull. It was the bull which Good had missed. It was coming charging right at them, but we could not fire at the elephant as we were scared that we might shoot Good or Khiva.

Then, just as they were about sixty yards from us, Good slipped and fell down. He was right in the path of the wounded elephant. We gasped and ran as fast as we could towards him, our hearts in our mouths. In three seconds, everything would have been over. The elephant towered over Good about to trample him. We were nowhere near them to be able to save Good or even distract the elephant for that matter. It was at this moment of need that help was unexpectedly delivered. Good was as good as done for, however, Khiva saved the day by throwing his spear at the elephant. His aim was perfect; it was straight into the elephant's face.

Nothing could have prepared us for what was about to happen. We watched in amazement as the spear got stuck just below the elephant's trunk, on

his neck. With a scream of pain, the brute seized Khiva and hurled him onto the ground. Then, he placed one huge foot on his body around the middle, twined its trunk around Khiva's upper body and tore him in two!

We were horrified at the scene unfurling in front of us and we fired again and again, till the elephant fell down dead. As for Good, he rose and wrung his hands over the brave man who had given his life to save him.

Umbopa stood silently by Khiva's remains, saying, "He died like a man."

# Chapter Five

# Our March

We had killed nine elephants and it took us two days to cut out the tusks. After burying Khiva and the tusks in the sands (to keep them safe), we restarted our journey. Soon, we reached the last fertile spot. Now all that stretched in front of us was the vast and dreaded desert.

Our camps were pitched by the evening under Good's supervision. I took Sir Henry with me to the top of the slope, where we could see the faint blue outlines of Solomon's Mines.

I said, "There is a wall around Solomon's Mines, but God alone knows if we shall ever be able to climb it."

"We will," Sir Henry said confidently.

Umbopa was leading the way. He was also looking at the far-off mountains.

Suddenly, he asked Sir Henry, "To reach there, you have to cross the vast desert, go past the snow-filled mountains and further beyond that. No one knows what lies there. Why, Incubu? Why do you want to go there?"

Incubu was the native name given to Sir Henry, meaning "elephant" in Zulu.

"Umbopa," answered Sir Henry, "I would go there and just about anywhere to find my brother."

"That is so, Incubu. A Hottentot I met on the road told me that a white man, who had eyes like yours, went out into the desert two years ago towards those mountains. He went with one servant and a hunter called Jim. But they never returned."

Sir Henry said, "If George wanted to do something, he did it. If he meant to cross the mountains, I am quite sure that he has crossed them, unless an accident prevented him or worse, killed him."

Umbopa laughed and said, "It seems to me that we are alike, Incubu. I also seek a brother over the mountains."

Suspicious, I asked Umbopa, "What do you mean? What do you know of those mountains?"

"I know just a little. The land beyond is strange. It is a land of witchcraft and beautiful things; a land of brave people and streams, snowy peaks, and a great white road. I have heard of it. If we survive, we will see it."

Seeing the shadow of doubt that lay heavily upon my face, Umbopa said, "I'm only telling you what I know. Death lurks in those mountains. It would be wise to turn back."

I was sure there was something else that Umbopa was not telling us, but I did not press further. On the next day, we dismissed our bearers. Then, we collected our elephant rifles and other heavier weapons, and loaded them.

We made arrangements with an old native to keep our other weapons till we returned.

I told the native that when we returned, even if one of those things was missing, I would kill him and his people using witchcraft. He believed me.

Then, we arranged our travelling kit. The kit was small but consisted of three Express rifles, Winchester repeating rifles, ammunition, water bottles, blankets, sun dried game flesh, mixed beads for gifts and medicine. We also included knives, a compass, matches, a pocket filter, tobacco, a trowel, a bottle of brandy and clothes.

We prayed and then we started. We were guided by the distant mountains and old Jose da Silvestre's chart. Considering that it was three centuries old, it was not a very wise thing to rely on, but our success depended upon it.

We began silently. The karoo bushes caught our feet, sand filled our boots and we had to stop to empty them every now and then, but we made fair progress. We rested briefly. But soon

the sun was fully up and it was impossible for us to travel.

After travelling for about sixty miles from our starting point, we had to find a pool of water marked on the map or we would all die.

I was worried that even if we did find the pool, it could be completely dry!

When we saw a little pit that offered shade from the sun, we dragged ourselves there. We crept into it, drank a few sips of water from our bottles and soon, we were sound asleep. It was 3 pm before we woke up.

Our bearers refused to come any further into the desert. They had accompanied us this far after a lot of convincing. All of us–Sir Henry, Good, Ventvogel, Umbopa and I–took a hearty drink. We refilled our empty water-bottles from the gourds that the natives had carried with them and started on our journey again.

It was an even more lonely and desolate walk, for we saw nothing living.

Every day at sunrise, we halted and once the moon rose, we trudged on wearily till sunrise. Tired, we drank a little and flung ourselves down on the sand. Soon we were all asleep. This time, we didn't find a sheltering pit to guard us from the glare of the sun.

At about 7 am, we woke up and felt that we were sitting inside an oven. There was not a bit of shelter to be found for miles and miles.

"What is to be done?" asked Sir Henry. "We can't stand this for long."

We looked at each other blankly. Good said, "We must dig a hole, get in it and cover ourselves with the karoo bushes."

We set to work with the trowel that we had brought with us. We crept inside the hole and covered ourselves with the shrub. However, this gave us little shelter from the burning sun.

The heat was unbearable. By about 3 pm we could bear it no longer. After taking a few more sips from our diminishing water supply, we staggered forward again, continuing our journey.

We must have covered some fifty miles of the wilderness. As per old da Silvestre's map, a spring should have been nearby.

At sunset, we rested again. Before we lay down, Umbopa pointed out a hillock about eight miles away, wondering what it was. As the moon rose, we marched again, dreadfully exhausted. At last, utterly worn out, we came to the foot of the queer hill. Here we halted and drank our last drops of water.

Just as I was falling asleep, I heard Umbopa say in Zulu, "If we cannot find water we shall all be dead before the moon rises tomorrow."

I shuddered.

## Chapter Six

# Water! Water!

It was close to dawn when I woke up with an intense thirst. We did not have a drop of water.

"If we do not find water, we will die," said Sir Henry.

"If we trust the old Dom's map, there should be some water nearby," I said.

But nobody said anything. None of them had a lot of faith in the accuracy of the map.

Suddenly, Ventvogel got up and started walking about with his eyes on the ground.

Then, he stopped short and pointed to the earth. He showed us fresh antelope prints and said, "Antelopes do not go far from water."

This little discovery put new life into us.

Then, Ventvogel sniffed the hot air and said, "I smell water." We were jubilant upon hearing this. We walked around the hillock and gazed about anxiously.

Sir Henry said, "It could be atop the hill!"

So we climbed up the sandy sides of the hillock. And there it was!

Though the water was dark and foul, we rushed towards it. We fell on our knees and drank it as though it were nectar fit for the gods. Once we were refreshed, we filled our bottles and ate our fill. Sated, we lay by the blessed pool and slept till noon.

The life-saving oasis provided us with as much water as we could hold and we were grateful to the long departed Da Silvestre for marking it accurately on the map.

We started off again at night. When the sun rose, we saw the majestic Suliman berg towering before us.

In the evening, we found ourselves upon the lowest slopes of Sheba's left breast. By now, we had again exhausted our water supply. Toiling further, we discovered that the mountains were volcanoes. Utterly exhausted, we continued to walk over lava clinkers.

Soon, we saw a ridge covered with dense green grass. Umbopa went further and started dancing and shouting like a maniac, waving something green.

"It is food and water, Macumazahn," he said. The green thing was a melon.

He found a patch of ripe melons growing in the wild. We were so thankful for this measly feast that we gorged on them. I even shot down a bird and we feasted on it. It was not much, but to us, after such a hard time trudging through the desert, it was a grand feast.

When we continued our march, we did not see any water or food for the next three days. We also noticed a change in the weather. The hot air was now starting to get replaced by a cool breeze.

The air had become a lot cooler. Our journey was taking its toll on us too. All of us were weak and the cold was worsening things for us. But the one person who was the most affected by the cold was Ventvogel.

Soon we reached the snow line and slowly we struggled up the incline of the snow. Just before sunset, we found ourselves exactly under the peak of Sheba's left breast.

"I say," gasped Good, "we ought to be somewhere near that cave the old gentleman wrote about.

Suddenly Umbopa caught my arm.

"Look!" He said, pointing straight ahead, at what appeared to be a hole in the snow.

"It is the cave!" Cried Umbopa.

We rushed towards it and settled inside. We were right on time, because minutes later, the sun went down.

We could not be more glad for the shelter we had found. The cave wasn't very big and we huddled ourselves together for warmth. The cold

was too intense to allow us to sleep. Ventvogel was resting behind me and I could hear his teeth chattering all night.

I heard him give a deep sigh and all of a sudden his teeth stopped chattering. He seemed to grow colder and colder, till at last, his body felt like ice.

At length, when sunlight filled the cave, we saw Ventvogel sitting there amongst us, stone dead and frozen. He had died in the night when I had heard him sighing. Shocked beyond measure, we let the corpse sit there, its arms clasped about its knees.

Suddenly, I heard someone exclaim and turned my head. Sitting at the end of the cavern was a white man's corpse.

Foolishly, we ran outside the cave.

# Chapter Seven

# Solomon's Road

Once we were outside, we halted, feeling silly.

"I am going back," said Sir Henry. "Because it may be my brother."

We re-entered the cave and Sir Henry knelt down and peered closely at the face. "Thank God," he said, relieved, "it is not my brother."

I saw that the body was that of a tall, middle-aged man. He had aquiline features, grizzled hair and a long, black moustache. His yellow skin stretched over his bones. His clothing was in tatters around him, leaving the skeleton-like frame almost naked. Around his neck hung a yellow ivory crucifix.

"Who is this?" I asked.

"Why, it's the old Dom, Jose da Silvestra," said Good.

"Impossible," I gasped, "he died three hundred years ago."

Good explained, "a body does not decompose in the cold. Also, there are no animals here. "

I nodded.

"Look!" He said, stooping to pick up a queerly-shaped bone scraped at the end into a sharp point. "Here is the 'cleft bone' that Silvestra used to draw the map with."

I stared, completely appalled. I was imagining the last scene of the old Dom's drama; of a traveller dying of cold and starvation; and yet trying to tell the world the great secret that he had discovered.

"Let us go," said Sir Henry.

He took the crucifix around the Dom's neck and I took the bone pen. We could think of no better way to honour Venvogel than to place him beside the Dom. We crept out of the cave and into the welcome sunshine.

We resumed our path and came to the edge of the plateau, but we could not see what lay below us due to the morning fog.

As the fog cleared, I saw plenty of grass and a stream around six hundred yards below us. The sight filled us with joy and I quickly pointed it out to the others. We desperately needed food. We made our way down and hunted antelopes. We greedily ate the meat raw after cleaning it in the ice-cold water. Once satisfied, we began inspecting our surroundings.

Behind us towered Sheba's snowy breast and below us lay the most beautiful country. There were dense patches of lofty forest and a great river wound its silvery way. This expanse was surrounded by a wall of mountains. It was wonderful. Sir Henry said, "Isn't there something on the map about Solomon's Great Road?"

I nodded.

"Look!" said Sir Henry as he pointed a little to our right. We quickly made our way to the

SOLOMON'S ROAD

magnificent path, carrying with us some flesh we had cut off from the antelopes.

The road was cut out of solid rock and incredibly well kept. We were amazed at the workmanship. It was a sort of Roman road in a strange land. At one place, we came to a ravine about three hundred feet broad. Its vast gulf was bridged with huge blocks of stone. At another place, the road was cut in zig-zags out of the side of a precipice, and in a third, it tunnelled through the base of an intervening ridge.

By noon, we came across a grove of trees with enough wood to cook our meat. When we had eaten our fill, we lit our pipes and smoked, feeling at peace. I looked around for Good and saw him standing in the stream, wearing nothing but his flannel shirt.

His natural habits of extreme neatness had reasserted themselves. He had turned his attention to his chin where accumulated the scrub of ten day's beard. He had succeeded in getting the hair off the right side of his face and chin.

I saw a flash of light passing by his head.

Good and I turned towards it. Standing near Good was a group of men. They were very tall and brown-skinned. Some wore great plumes of black feathers and short cloaks of leopard skins. In front of them stood a boy of seventeen, his hand raised and body bent forward. It was evident that he had hurled the weapon.

Good was quick despite his fright and along with Sir Henry and Umbopa, he lifted his rifle threateningly. The men still advanced towards us. I realised that the men did not know what rifles were.

"Put down your guns!" I cried out to Sir Henry and Good. They obeyed. Walking to the front, I addressed the elderly man.

"Greetings," I said in Zulu, not knowing what language to try. To my surprise, I was understood.

"Greetings," answered the old man. "From where do you come? Who are you? And why are three of you white while the fourth one looks like

our mother's son?" He asked, pointing at Umbopa and staring curiously.

"We are strangers and we come in peace," I answered. "This man is our servant."

"If you are strangers, you must prepare to die, for no strangers may live in the land of Kukuanas!" He answered.

"What does he say?" asked Good.

"He says we're going to be killed," I answered.

"Oh, Lord!" Groaned Good and put his hand to his false teeth. Suddenly, the top set came down, after which they snapped back in place. It turned out to be the most fortunate move.

"AAAIIIEEE" yelled the dignified tribe of Kukuanas and stepped back in horror. "What's wrong?" I asked.

"It's his teeth," whispered Sir Henry excitedly. "Take them out, Good!"

He obeyed. The old man stepped forward, curious. "How is it, O strangers," he asked solemnly, pointing to Good, "that this fat man — whose body is clothed but whose legs are bare, who grows hair on one side of his face and not on the other, and who wears one shining and transparent eye — has teeth which move on their own?"

What happened next was a bit of drama. Good took out his teeth and put them back in.

The old man became fearful. He said slowly, "I see that you are spirits. Did every man born from a woman have hair on one side of his face and not on the other? Or one eye round and transparent? Or teeth which moved and melted away and grew again? Pardon us, my lords."

I jumped at the opportunity and said, "It is granted. We come from another world, though we are men like you. We come from the biggest star that shines at night."

I continued to lie, "This is not the reception expected for a man whose teeth come and go. We must avenge his insult by killing the man who threw the knife at him."

"Spare him, my lords," appealed the old man. "He is the king's son and I am his uncle. If anything befalls him, I will be blamed."

"Yes," put in the young man.

I thought that this was a good opportunity to trick them and save ourselves, so I went on. "You may doubt our power to avenge," I continued addressing the crowd.

"Do you see that buck?" I asked, pointing at an antelope grazing in the distance. "Tell me, do you think it is possible to kill it with just a noise?"

"It is not possible," the old man replied, looking at me doubtfully.

"I shall kill it," I said quietly. I was tensed, but I raised the rifle to shoot with a steady hand. I knew that our fate depended on my shot and I could not afford to miss. So I took a deep breath, aimed at the buck and pressed the trigger. It could have been my lucky day for the bullet hit the mark, killing the buck instantly. I smiled to myself triumphantly and turned around to observe the group.

What happened next was a sight to see. The men grew alarmed. A groan of terror burst from the group before us and they held up their arms in shock!

The old gentleman trembled. "Listen, O children of the Stars, of the Shining Eye and Movable Teeth, who roar in thunder and slay from afar. I am Infadoos, son of Kafa, once the king of the Kukuana people.

This youth is Scragga, son of Twala, the great king. Twala is the husband of a thousand wives, lord paramount of the Kukuanas, keeper of the great road, terror of his enemies, student of the Black Arts. Twala is the Black, the Terrible."

"So," I shrugged, "lead us to Twala. We do not talk to underlings."

The old man made a deep obeisance and murmured the words, "Koom Koom." Afterwards, I discovered that this was their royal salute. Infadoos turned and addressed his people. At once, they picked up all our goods and carried everything for us, except our guns which they refused to touch. They even seized Good's clothes, including his trousers which were lying folded on a tree.

Good wanted to put them on and a loud argument followed.

"Nay, my lord," said Infadoos, "would my lord cover up his beautiful white legs from the eyes of servants? Have we offended my lord that he should do so?"

"Look, Good," said Sir Henry to captain Good. "You have appeared in this country in a certain character and you must live it up. It will never do for you to put on trousers again."

"Yes," I agreed, "and with whiskers on one side of your face and not on the other. If you change any of these things, the people will begin to suspect us and we will be killed."

Good sighed and said no more.

# Chapter Eight

# We Enter Kukuanaland

All afternoon, as we walked, I made an effort to learn more about this land and its people.

"Infadoos," I asked, "who made this road?"

"It was made, my lord, during an old time. Nobody knows who made it, how and when."

"When did the Kukuana people come here?"

"My lord, the race came down here like the breath of a storm ten thousand thousand moons ago, from the great lands which lie there beyond," he said, pointing to the north.

"We are many. When Twala, the King, calls the regiments, their plumes cover the plains as far as the eye can see. But it's been a long time since we had a war. The last one was a civil war."

"How is that?"

"My lord, our King, Kafa, had twins named Imotu and Twala. Our custom is to kill the weaker child, but Kafa's wife hid Twala. I was born later to the King Kafa and I am Twala's younger half brother.

Kafa, our father, died when we were growing up. Imotu was made the king in his place. For a time, Imotu reigned. He had a son named Ignosi, but when the baby was three years old, Imotu fell ill. A famine fell upon the land and the people were miserable. Then Gagool, the wise and terrible woman-who-does-not-die, made a proclamation to the people, saying, 'The King Imotu is no king.' She brought out the hidden twin Twala, my half brother and twin brother, to the King Imotu.

She showed that he was marked with the sacred snake as all kings are marked when born. 'Behold your true king,' she said.

When Imotu came out to investigate, Twala killed him.

Imotu's wife and child fled. Twala became the king and crushed those who resisted him. Imotu's wife and Ignosi died while trying to flee Kukuanaland."

"If Ignosi had lived, he would be the true king of the Kukuana people?" I asked.

"That is so, my lord," Infadoos replied.

Soon, Infadoos pointed to a vast collection of huts surrounded by a fence and a great ditch on a plain beneath us. "It is there that we shall sleep tonight," he said, sending a runner ahead to warn the people of the kraal of our arrival.

When we arrived within two miles of the Kraal, we saw company after company of men marching towards us. Each company comprised about three hundred strong men. They were the most magnificent set of warriors I had ever seen. They were tall, mature veterans, each carrying an iron shield and three heavy knives called "tollas". With flashing spears and waving

plumes, these men would take their appointed place. As we approached, a signal was given by the commanding officer. Every spear was raised into the air and three hundred warriors roared the royal salute of "Koom". As soon as we had passed, the company formed behind us and followed us towards the kraal.

Finally, the whole regiment of the "Greys" — named so because of their white shields — was marching behind us. We entered the kraal, which was exceedingly well laid out. It had a central pathway which was intersected at right angles by other pathways, forming blocks for the huts. The huts were beautifully thatched, dome-shaped structures with verandahs.

All along the pathway stood hundreds of women. They were well-bred and fascinated by Good's beautiful white legs. Good was greatly embarrassed by the incident.

We entered the hut that was prepared for us. Once we settled in, we asked Infadoos and Scragga to join us. Scragga's awe for us started

wearing off when he saw that we ate, drank and slept just like ordinary men.

After supper we took out our pipes and lit them; a proceeding that filled Infadoos and Scragga with astonishment. Infadoos informed us that Twala was at Loo, preparing for the great annual feast, which was to be held in the first week of June.

"At this gathering, all the regiments are brought up and paraded before the king; and the great annual witch-hunt takes place," said Infadoos with a sigh.

Soon, he left us alone while we slept peacefully on comfortable beds. It had been a while since we had beds to sleep on, so we fell asleep almost instantly.

# Chapter Nine

# Twala the King

The next morning, we were on our way to Loo. Good got upset that our luggage, which included his trousers, was sent ahead. It took us two days to reach Loo. Along the way, we were overtaken by over thousands of warriors, all hurrying towards Loo.

The adventures of the past days did not deter us from inquiring about Sir Henry's brother. In each case, the answer was the same. "Only one white man ever made it to Kukuanaland."

Loo was located in the centre of a fertile valley. It was the largest kraal we had ever seen.

Through the centre was a river, dividing it into two portions. The river was bridged in several places. Sixty or seventy miles away, stood three great snow-capped mountains that looked a lot like perfect triangles.

Infadoos explained, "These mountains are known among the Kukuanas as the 'Three Witches'. They are full of caves and there is a great pit between them. It is in there that the wise men of olden times would go to get whatever it was they came for to this country. It is there that our kings are buried. We call it the 'Place of Death'."

"I have heard," I probed, "that the wise men came to these mountains to find bright stones and yellow iron."

"My lord is wise," Infadoos raised his hand and answered coldly. "You must speak with Gagool the old, who is also wise," he said and went away.

I pointed the mountains to the others and said, "There lie Solomon's diamond mines."

Umbopa was standing with us. He said, "Yes, Macumazahn, the diamonds are there and you shall have them." He laughed and walked ahead.

Soon, we were at the gate of a little group of huts which surrounded a small courtyard of powdered limestone. These were to be our "poor" quarters. We ate, drank and slept. We woke up refreshed, expecting to meet the king.

The king lived in a very large hut that was on about six acres of land. His wives' huts were along the perimeter. It was a grand spectacle to see warriors filling the open ground and standing perfectly still. Soon, we were seated on stools placed in front of the large hut.

A gigantic figure, wearing a crown of skull and horns, stepped out and sat on a throne. He had thick lips, a flat nose and one eye. His expression was cruel and he was ugly to look at. He wore a magnificent hide around his waist. In his right hand was a huge spear adorned with an enormous uncut diamond.

Scragga appeared and stood behind the king. When the king raised his great spear, eight thousand voices repeated the royal salute "KOOM" thrice. It ended in a deathly silence. This was broken by a soldier dropping his shield. The king looked at him and commanded, "You! Come here!"

The young man stood before Twala.

"What hast thou to say for thyself?"

"It was by chance, Your Majesty" he murmured.

"It is a chance for which you must pay."

The king signalled Scragga, who waved his spear and struck home. The soldier dropped dead. Sir Henry swore loudly, boiling with rage. I held him back saying, "Not now, Sir Henry. Get a hold on yourself. Our lives depend on it."

Four men lifted the body and carried it away.

Then, Twala addressed us. "Greetings, white people," he said.

"Greetings, King of Kukuanas," I answered.

"White people, you said you come from the Stars," he said. Pointing to Umbopa, he asked, "does he also come from the Stars?"

"There are people of your colour in the heavens above. Do not question matters that are too high for you, King Twala."

"Ye speak with a loud voice," Twala answered. "Remember that the Stars are far off and you are here. What if I did to you the same that I did to this man here?"

"O King," I said, "walk carefully over hot stones or you may burn your feet. Have you not heard about the kind of men that we are?"

"They have told me, but I believe them not. Kill me a man from among these warriors."

"No," I answered; "we do not kill like that. Give me an ox and I will strike it dead."

"Nay," laughed the King, "kill a man."

"So be it," I answered coolly. "Send Scragga to the fence."

This suggestion did not please Twala. "Let a young ox be driven in," he suggested instead.

"Now, Sir Henry," I said loudly, "I want you to take the shot. I don't want Twala to think that I am the only magician among us."

Sir Henry accordingly took his shot and, to the astonishment of the crowd, the ox fell dead.

A wizened monkey-like figure was standing behind the King all this while, covered in a shroud. Soon, it came forward. It threw back the covering from its face to reveal an old woman whose face had shrunk. She had deep wrinkles and looked like a corpse, except for a pair of black eyes. Her eyes were full of fire and intelligence.

It was Gagool, the witch-finder, the woman Infadoos had called the kingmaker of the civil war. In a thin, piercing voice she said, "Blood, blood, blood, blood! Everywhere I see it, I smell it and I taste it."

She turned towards us and said, "White men, do you seek a lost one? I must warn you, you shall not find him here."

She turned to Umbopa and said "You look familiar. Remove your girdle."

However, as soon as she said this, she convulsed into epileptic fits and had to be carried inside.

We decided to gift the King with a gun.

"We give this magic tube to you," I told him, "but remember, you shall kill no man with it. If you use it against a man, it shall kill you."

The King was impressed and accepted my gift of the express rifle with reverence and awe.

Twala gave us exquisitely crafted chain-mail shirts, usually reserved for the royal family. Then, he said, "White people, you may go now. Please come for the great dance."

Accompanied by Infadoos, we returned to our kraal.

# Chapter Ten

# The Witch Hunt

On reaching our hut, I told Infadoos, "it seems to us that King Twala is a cruel man."

"It is so, my lords. Alas! The land groans at the cruelties of King Twala. You shall see at the great witch hunt, when many will be slain. No life is safe. Perhaps, I too shall be killed. As yet I have been spared because I am skilled in war and the soldiers are fond of me."

"Why don't the people bring him down?"

"My lords, he is the king. If he were killed, Scragga, his son, would take his place. The heart of Scragga is blacker than his father's. If Imotu had never been slain or if Ignosi, his son, had

lived, it might have been otherwise; but they are both dead."

"How do you know that Ignosi is dead?" asked Umbopa, astonishing all of us.

"What do you mean, boy?" asked Infadoos.

"I'm Ignosi, the rightful king of Kukuanaland!" Umbopa announced, revealing the picture of a great snake tattooed around his stomach.

"My mother," explained Umbopa, "fled the Kukuanaland. She travelled for many years into a land of wonders and lived among the white men. When she died, I promised to return to the land of my fathers. After years, I got a chance to come here with the white men."

On hearing this, Infadoos fell upon his knees. "Koom! Koom!" He praised. "It is the king! Ignosi, I'm your servant till the day I die. I will speak to some of the chiefs and bring them to see you. Together we shall help you overthrow King Twala."

"Thank you, Infadoos. And you," he said, turning towards us, "will you help me?"

I translated his question for Sir Henry and Good. We all agreed to stand by Ignosi.

I said to him, "We will help. But you must help us find Sir Henry's brother."

"That I will do," answered Ignosi.

The next day, when we went for the witch hunt, we decided to wear the chain-mail shirts. Infadoos warned us, "Anyone's life could be in danger, including your own. This is when Twala used his executioners and the crones under Gagool to single out the ones he wanted to kill."

On arriving, we found twenty thousand men packed in. This was only a third of Twala's army. Infadoos said, "Many will be killed today."

We sat on stools near the great hut. Soon, King Twala, Scragga his son, Gagool, and the executioners with spears and kerries in their hands came out.

The King seated himself upon the centre stool and the others stood behind him.

"Greetings, white lords," Twala cried. "You shall see a glorious show today."

The King signalled for the show to begin. From a far point of the circle, a lone voice began a wailing song and company after company picked it up, turning it into love song and then a majestic, swelling war chant. It ended in one heart-breaking wail, followed by silence.

Suddenly, we heard a pattering of feet. Strange, awful figures came running towards us. We saw that these were aged women. Their hair was white and their faces were painted in stripes of white and yellow. They wore human bones around their waists and each held a small forked wand in her hand. They stopped before Gagool, who cried out, "Isanusis! Are your senses awake? Can you smell blood? Are you ready to do justice? Then go! See the slayers. Go!"

With a wild yell, Gagool's horrid crones headed for the circle of human beings. The Isanusis began to dance wildly near the warriors. They bent and twisted in an unholy dance, appearing to be seized by the power to sniff out evil in the hearts and minds of men.

Then, suddenly, in a moment, the crone's sticks would touch a target. It was a death sentence.

We watched helplessly. I turned my head away and gazed at the moon, Sir Henry's teeth ground together so hard that I could hear them over the shrieking. I thought that they would splinter.

Later, when I spoke to Good, he told me that he had closed his eyes, but they seemed to open at the worst possible moment, showing him horrors that he couldn't forget easily.

Around 10:30 pm, the witch-finders gathered together, apparently exhausted. The King began counting. Around hundred such warriors were killed. We thought that the night was over, but it was not so.

Gagool rose and staggered into the open space. She started muttering, then she began running and pointing. Gradually, she came near us and pointed at Umbopa. In a strange, shaky voice, she said, "Kill him, kill him, he is full of evil; this stranger. Slay him, O King."

There was a pause. Everyone's eyes moved between Umbopa and the King, wondering what would happen next.

I took advantage of this silence.

"I apologise, O King," I called out, rising to my feet, "but this man shall not die. He is under my protection. But if anyone lays a finger on him, they will die."

"Gagool, mother of the witch-finders, has smelt him out. He must die," declared Twala.

"Seize him!" Twala roared to the executioners. They advanced menacingly towards us.

"Stand back!" I shouted. "If you touch one hair on his head, your king dies."

I pointed my gun at the king. Sir Henry and Good also drew their pistols. Sir Henry pointed his pistol at the leading executioner and Good took a deliberate aim at Gagool.

Twala winced visibly and said, "Put away your magic tubes. I agree to spare him. The dance has ended. You may leave."

In an instant, the regiments went out of the kraal in complete silence. They marched out quickly, clearing the place in no time. We, too, joined the troops and returned to our hut.

"If I had any doubts about helping Umbopa to rebel against that king," Good spoke at last. "You may rest assured that they are gone now. It was a close call, Ignosi. But where is Infadoos?"

"I am grateful, Bougwan," said Umbopa, "and I shall not forget. As for Infadoos, he will be here by-and-by. We must wait for him."

# Chapter Eleven

# We Give a Sign

It had been decided that Infadoos would bring the other chiefs to seek their help. True to his word, at around dawn, Infadoos brought over half-dozen stately looking chiefs to meet Ignosi.

Infadoos said, "I have told them all that I have seen and heard. Now let them also see your sacred snake and hear your story."

So Ignosi repeated his story for all the chiefs. But the chiefs wanted more. They wanted to see some magical sign to prove to their people that he really was their true king. Perplexed, I turned to Sir Henry and Good, and explained the situation to them.

"I think that I have it," said Good. He asked the chiefs to wait out and pulled out an almanac when they left.

"Tomorrow is the 4th of June. There is a lunar eclipse that will be clearly visible in Africa. The eclipse would begin at about 10 pm tomorrow night and last for an hour and a half. That should be the magical sign for the chiefs. Tell them that we will darken the moon tomorrow night," said Good.

The idea was a splendid one. Only, if it did not work, our prestige would be lost, along with Ignosi's chance of becoming the king.

We called the chiefs back inside. I said, "Great men of the Kukuanas, listen to us. We do not like to display our power. But we are angered against Twala's cruelty and Isanusi Gagool's wickedness. So we have decided to break the rule and give such a sign as all men may see. Tomorrow night, about two hours before midnight, we will cause the moon to be eaten up by darkness for an hour and a half. It shall be a sign that Ignosi is indeed

King of the Kukuanas. If we do this thing, will you be satisfied?"

"Yes, my lords," answered the old chief. Infadoos wore a satisfied smile on his face. He outlined a plan. "Tonight, many girls will dance. Twala will pick the fairest and she shall be killed by Scragga as a sacrifice to the 'Silent Ones'. My lords, if you save the maiden's life, the people will believe you."

"Two miles from Loo," went on Infadoos, "lies a hill where my regiment is stationed. There are three more regiments that can be moved there. After you darken the moon, I will take you there to keep you safe."

We agreed and Infadoos left with the chiefs.

"My friends," asked Ignosi. "Can you really do this wonderful thing?"

"I believe we can."

"I have learned that English gentlemen tell no lies," he answered. "I will repay you if we live through this."

"Ignosi," said Sir Henry, "promise me that if you become the king, you will stop the practice of witch hunting and a trial will take place before condemning a man."

"I promise, Incubu," answered Ignosi smiling.

Later that evening, we went to Twala's kraal for the "great annual dance" of girls. Once again, we put on the chain-mail shirts that the King had given us before going out. This time, we didn't have to be reminded how dangerous it was.

Now, in the open space, instead of the grim warriors, were Kukuana girls. Each girl was crowned with a wreath of flowers, and was holding a palm leaf in one hand and a white arum lily in the other. King Twala, who was already seated there with his entourage, greeted us cordially upon our arrival.

"Let the dance begin," cried out Twala, gesturing with his hands.

The flower-crowned girls sprang forward, dancing round and round. At last they paused, and a beautiful young woman sprang out of the

ranks. She began to dance in front of us with grace and vigour. When she was exhausted, another took her place, then another and another. But none of them matched the first girl in grace, skills or even something as simple as attractiveness.

"Who is the fairest, white man?" King Twala asked us.

"The first girl" I said, completely mesmerised by her beauty and elegance.

"I agree" said the King.

I had forgotten for a moment that this girl would be offered as sacrifice. "Why, O King?" I asked the King with difficulty when it dawned upon me that I had chosen her for the sacrifice. "Why reward the fairest girl with death?"

"It is our custom and our duty to the figures that dwell in those mountains. If I fail to put the fairest girl to death today, misfortune would fall upon me and my house," replied Twala.

He commanded the guards, "Bring her here. Scragga, sharpen your spear."

Two of the men walked towards her. Before she could even attempt to run, she was caught and brought before us.

"What is thy name, girl?" Gagool walked up to her and stood in front of her.

"Oh, mother," answered the girl, trembling and falling upon her knees. "My name is Foulata. But mother, why must I die? I have done no wrong! Why can't I be spared?"

"You should feel honoured that you are chosen," replied Gagool. "You must die as a sacrifice for the old ones in the mountains."

The girl, Foulata, was in agony. She begged, "I want to see my parents. I want to marry and have children. Have mercy on me." But her desperate pleas had no effect on either Gagool or Twala.

Seeing the futility of her pleas, she ran to Good and flung herself on him and said, "Oh, white father from the Stars!" She cried, "protect me! Save me from these cruel people. Save me from this terrible fate."

"Don't worry, I'll look after you," said Good.

Twala turned and signalled for Scragga to kill Foulata. "Now's your time," whispered Sir Henry.

"I am waiting for that eclipse," I answered. "I have had my eye on the moon for the last half-hour and it will soon begin."

"Well, you must risk it now."

"King," I said. "Let the girl go."

Twala got angry. "Are you mad? Be careful or you shall get killed too. Who are you to interfere in my affairs? Scragga, kill her! Guards, seize these men."

His men started towards us. Sir Henry, Good, and Ignosi readied their rifles.

"Stop!" I shouted boldly. "We, the white men from the Stars, say so. Come closer and we will put out the moon, and plunge the land in darkness." My threat halted them.

"Hear him!" Piped Gagool. "Hear the liar who says that he will put out the moon. Let him do it or the girl shall be speared along with him and those who are like him."

Despaired, I glanced up at the moon and to my joy, saw that the eclipse had begun.

Then, I lifted my hand solemnly towards the sky, followed by Sir Henry and Good, quoting from various texts. As the eclipse progressed, deep gasps of fear rose from the crowd.

"Look, oh King!" I cried. "Look, Gagool! Look, people and tell us if we are liars! The moon grows black before your eyes! Soon, there will be darkness in the hour of the full moon. You have asked for a sign and we are giving it to you."

The crowd was petrified. Even the King turned pale, but Gagool kept her courage.

"It will pass," she cried. "I have seen this before; the shadow will pass."

The eclipse continued to progress. In the next ten minutes, everything grew as still as death.

"The moon is dying. The white wizards have killed the moon," yelled Scragga at last. "We shall all die in the dark."

Filled with anger, he hurled his spear at Sir Henry. But the spear rebounded on the chain-mail shirt that Sir Henry was wearing. Sir Henry picked up the spear and hurled it at Scragga, killing him instantly.

The crowd panicked and started running amok. The King and his guards fled for the huts, followed by some of the chiefs and Gagool. Only some chiefs and Foulata were left.

"Chiefs," I spoke to them, "we have given you the sign. If you are satisfied, let us leave. Let us cover ourselves in the darkness."

"Come," said Infadoos. We followed him along with the chiefs and Foulata. By then, the moon was completely engulfed in darkness.

# Chapter Twelve

# Before the Battle

Since the chiefs and Infadoos knew the paths well, we easily crossed the town to reach the large, flat-topped grassland. Here, a regiment of Greys was already stationed. We were astonished to find two men waiting with our belongings.

"I sent for them," explained Infadoos, "and for these." He lifted up Good's long-lost trousers. Good was so delighted, he wore them instantly.

"Surely my lord will not hide his beautiful white legs!" Pleaded Infadoos regretfully, but Good insisted. Infadoos stepped forward to explain the cause of rebellion to the troops. He narrated the story of King Imotu's murder and

Ignosi's survival. He also pointed out how the people suffered under Twala's cruel rule.

Pointing to us, he said that the White Lords from the Stars had led the real king of Kukuanas, Ignosi, out of his exile. The white men had also shown them a sign from the heavens and saved Foulata with their magic. He explained that the white men were prepared to assist them to overthrow Twala and setup the rightful king, Ignosi, in his place.

Then, Ignosi stepped forward.

He reiterated what his uncle Infadoos had said. In conclusion, he said, "O chiefs, captains, soldiers and people, now you must make a choice between me and he who sits upon my throne. I am indeed the king and these chiefs can tell you. They have seen the snake around my middle. If I were not the king, would these white men help me with their magic?" He pointed at us.

"I am the king," went on Ignosi, standing confident and straight.

"If there is any man among you who says that it is not so, let him fight me and his blood shall be a sign that I tell you the truth," declared Ignosi.

Nobody seemed inclined to respond to this heroic cry. Ignosi continued, "I promise that when I sit upon the seat of my fathers, bloodshed shall cease in the land; witch hunts will stop and justice will prevail throughout the land. Have you chosen?"

"We have chosen, O King," came the answer.

"It is well," said Ignosi.

Later, we held a council with the commanders. We would be attacked by over thirty-five thousand men, so we set about planning.

Ignosi consulted with me on his war plans. We began setting up our defences. The paths up the hill were made impregnable by piling up boulders. More boulders were collected at various spots to be rolled down upon the advancing enemy. Then, just before sundown, we saw a small company of men advancing towards us with a palm leaf. "Greetings!" cried one of them, "The

king sends his greeting to those who wish to fight against him."

"Speak," I said.

"These are the king's words. Surrender to the king's mercy before tragedy befalls you. I will have mercy and be satisfied with a little blood. One in every ten shall die, the rest shall go free. But the white man who slew Scragga, my son, and the black man, his servant, who wants my throne, and Infadoos my brother, who brew the rebellion against me, shall die by torture as an offering to the 'Silent Ones'."

I answered loudly, so that all the soldiers might hear. "Go back to Twala and say that we, Ignosi, the veritable King, Incubu, Bougwan, and Macumazahn, the wise ones from the Stars, Infadoos, the chiefs and people gathered here refuse to surrender. Before the sun has gone down twice, Twala's corpse shall stiffen at his gate. Ignosi shall reign in his stead."

The herald laughed loudly and left. That night, we continued our preparations.

It was rather late when we retired to our huts.

"Sir Henry," I said, "I am scared."

Sir Henry laughed and said, "I have heard you say that before, Quatermain. I'd rather be killed fighting than any other way. Now that there is little to no chance of us finding my brother, the idea of dying is easier for me. We may be fortunate and we may succeed."

After this, we went to sleep.

At dawn, Infadoos woke us up. We rose and dressed for the fray, each putting on his chain-mail shirt as an armour. Sir Henry, however, dressed himself like a native warrior, including a leopard skin cloak, a plume of black ostrich feathers, a moocha of ox-tails, a heavy battle axe, a round shield and throwing knives, along with his revolver.

Good and I took a spear, a shield, a couple of tollas, a revolver and a huge plume, which I pinned into my hat. In addition to all this, we had our rifles and carried a good amount of ammunition with us.

We joined Infadoos and his regiment. They were watching the king's army creep out of Loo. Twala's force was split three ways: one to the right, one to the left and the third directly towards us.

"Ah," said Infadoos, "they are going to attack us on all three sides at once."

Quickly, orders were sent to the various regiments to prepare to receive the separate onslaughts.

# Chapter Thirteen

# The Attack

Sir Henry suggested that we should first attack the enemy commanders. I agreed. At the first opportunity, he lifted his spear angrily and hurled it. To our dismay, it hit the commander's companion. Alarmed, the commander started running towards his men. I shot at him. He threw up his arms and fell face down. Our regiments cheered, this was an omen of success.

Sir Henry and Good also began to fire and killed eight men. We fired steadily from our rifles. However, this had little effect on the vast army. On they stormed, shouting their war-cry, "Twala! Twala! Chiele! Chiele!"

"Ignosi! Ignosi! Chiele! Chiele!" Chanted our people. The enemy were quite close now and knives were being hurled back and forth. Soon, our first and second line of defence merged with the third. By this time, we had wounded and killed many of Twala's army. They were unable to break through our third line.

Sir Henry watched the struggle. Then, without a word he rushed into the battle with Good. The soldiers cried "Nanzia Incubu! Nanzia Unkungunklovo!" Which meant, here's the Elephant! I stood where I was.

The men fought with splendid gallantry. A messenger informed us that the attack on the left was repulsed. However, to my horror, the attack on the right had intensified.

Ignosi issued rapid orders. In no time, I joined the fray! I was timid but I had risen to the occasion. All I can remember is the dreadful clash of shields. Shortly, someone knocked me down.

When I woke up, I found Good bending over me, offering me sips of water. Giving an update, he said, "The enemy is repulsed for now. The loss is heavy. Two thousand of our men are killed and wounded, and they must have lost three."

We looked around and found Sir Henry, Ignosi, Infadoos and a few other chiefs in deep consultation. Sir Henry still held the battle-axe in his hand.

Seeing me, he exclaimed, "Here you are, Quatermain! It seems that though we have beaten them off the attack, Twala is now receiving large reinforcements. He intends to starve us. Moreover, Infadoos says that the water supply has given out."

"My lord Macumazahn," said Infadoos. "We have no water and little food. What shall we do? We must choose between three things: we may languish like a starving lion in his den; we may strive to break away towards the north; or we may launch ourselves at Twala's throat. Ignosi's word will be final as he is the king, but we want to know your opinion. What do you think we should do?"

After consultations with Good and Sir Henry, I said, "We must initiate an attack at once. It is our best and only shot."

This opinion was favourably received. Ignosi told Infadoos, "Towards evening, we will advance towards the narrow passage. Twala will see our men and send his forces there. But the spot is narrow and his regiment can come against us only one at a time. You must go ahead with your regiment, I will follow with Macumazahn." Infadoos agreed, even though he knew that his regiment might not survive this attack.

"While Twala's soldiers will be busy fighting Infadoos and his regiment," continued Ignosi, "one-third of our men shall creep along the right side of the hill and fall upon Twala's flank. Another one-third shall creep along the left side and attack Twala's left flank. I, with the remaining men, will charge Twala's forces from the front. If we are fortunate, we shall win."

Accordingly, our eighteen thousand men began to make their preparations.

Just as we finished discussing our battle plans, Good spoke up.

"Goodbye, fellows," he said. "I am off with the right wing, according to orders. I came to shake hands in case we don't meet again."

We shook hands in silence.

"I confess that I do not expect to see tomorrow's sun," said Sir Henry. "But I know that our men will fight till the end. Goodbye, old fellow. God bless you! Quatermain, I hope you will pull through and live to see the diamonds."

We shook hands and joined our respective regiments, preparing ourselves for the battle.

# Chapter Fourteen

# The Last Stand of the Greys

Ignosi delivered a motivating speech to the regiments. The men were charged and ready to fight. I had never seen such devotion to duty before.

The first set of Greys marched off. Ignosi followed and I went with his men.

Forty thousand enemy troops moved towards us. However, they hesitated when they discovered that only one regiment could advance into the gorge. Twala's army showed no eagerness to cross spears with the famous Greys regiment.

However, Twala himself arrived and the first regiment charged on his orders. The fight

began. It did not last long; the enemy's attacking lines grew thinner. Twala's regiment was destroyed. A third of the army of Greys was dead. The ground was covered by dead, dying and wounded human beings. Ignosi issued an order that the wounded enemy soldiers were not to be killed.

The remaining Greys silently awaited the next attack. Sir Henry was rearranging them. When the Greys were attacked again, the fighting was more intense and lasted longer. Only a third of the Greys survived. Again, they resumed their positions. Ignosi remained calm but I could bear it no longer, "Are we to stand here and see Twala slaughter our brothers?" I asked him.

Lifting his battle-axe, Ignosi gave the signal for us to advance. Soon, we were in a furious fight, shoulder to shoulder with Sir Henry.

Infadoos, the old warrior, was shouting orders to the remaining men and stepping forward to wherever the fighting was thickest. Sir Henry was also gallant, killing all who stood before him.

Suddenly there rose a cry of "Twala". He came forward and shouted, "Where are you, Incubu, who killed my son? See if you can kill me!" He stuck Sir Henry with his battle axe, bringing him down to his knees. Just then the regiments attacking us realised that they were being attacked from the right and the left. Twala was taken by surprise. In five minutes, the fate of the battle was decided. Only our regiments remained standing in the plain like a rock in the sea. Of the gallant three thousand four hundred Greys, only ninety-five remained.

"Men," said Infadoos calmly, "you have preserved the honour of your regiment. This day will be remembered by your grandchildren."

Then he shook Sir Henry's hand and said, "You are a great captain, Incubu. I have lived all my life among warriors and have known many a brave men, yet I've never seen a man like you."

At this moment, an officer informed Ignosi that Twala and his army had taken refuge in the town, but that they were thoroughly demoralised

and would surrender. Ignosi, after consulting us, sent a message to the defeated soldiers that he promised life and forgiveness to every soldier who would lay down his arms. When we entered Loo, thousands of dejected warriors stood along the road and saluted Ignosi as he passed. We marched straight to Twala's kraal. It was deserted, except for Twala and Gagool. We marched across towards Twala.

As we drew near, Twala mocked, "Hail, King!" He asked Ignosi bitterly, "With the white men's magic you have seduced my regiments and defeated my army. What will you do with me?"

"The same that you did to my father," answered Ignosi sternly.

"I accept; but I want to die fighting. Surely, you will not deny me that."

"It is granted," Ignosi told him sternly. I could see that he would make a great king. He was fierce and just. "Choose the soldier with whom you want to fight. I cannot fight you for a king fights only during a war."

"Incubu," said Twala, addressing Sir Henry. "Shall we finally put an end to our fight today or shall I call you a coward?"

"No," Ignosi spoke hastily to Twala. "You shall not fight with Incubu, he is my white brother."

Then, laying his hand affectionately on Sir Henry's arm, Ignosi said, "You have fought enough during this battle and if you die at his hands it would break my heart."

"I will fight him," declared Sir Henry. He did not like being called a coward by Twala, who was smugly watching us talk.

"For Heaven's sake," I entreated, trying to knock some sense into Sir Henry's thick head. Don't risk your life against that of a desperate man. You have done a lot for the battle already."

As I picked up the battle axe, suddenly beginning to wonder if I had bitten off more than I could chew, Sir Henry stopped me. I looked at him in question, he remained sullenly silent for a few seconds and finally spoke, "I will fight him,"

Then he took the axe from me and confidently stepped forward.

Twala laughed savagely and stepped towards Sir Henry. They began to circle round each other, their battle-axes raised, ready to strike any minute. We held our breaths and watched them, hoping for the best.

Each one was waiting for the other to make the first move and so for a few long seconds, nothing happened. Then suddenly Sir Henry sprang forward and struck a powerful blow at Twala, who stepped aside to shield himself from it. The fighting between them was intense and fierce, as they were well matched. Twala was extremely aggressive in his fighting; he fought as his life depended on it.

Sir Henry's chain mail protected him from Twala's knife. Finally, after a long, nail-biting fight, Sir Henry managed to get a hold on Twala's axe and struck it hard on his neck. Twala fell down with a mighty thud and breathed his last.

Everyone rejoiced. The battle was finally over. Twala was well and truly defeated. Sir Henry looked relieved, almost as though he had doubted his own victory.

I walked up to Twala's corpse, and loosened the diamond that was embedded in a belt from Twala's forehead and handed it to Ignosi.

"Take it," I said, "O King of the Kukuanas! You are king by birth and victory. You deserve to wear this."

Ignosi took it from me and bound the diadem upon his brows. Then, he said, "Our rebellion has ended in victory. In the morning, the oppressors had arisen, binding on their harness and they came ready to war. They came up against me, to kill me. But, they were killed. Now let all be well. Rejoice, my people, rejoice!"

Hearing this, all the people cheered Ignosi, declaring, "You are the king!"

# Chapter Fifteen

# Good Falls Sick

Sir Henry and Good were carried into the hut. Sir Henry was heavily wounded and Good had lost a lot of blood in the battlefield.

Foulata had constituted herself as our handmaiden. She helped us in removing our chain-mail shirts. She applied a native herbal ointment made from pounded green leaves on the bruises. She even fed us meals as we lay recovering in bed.

However, our wounds needed more attention. Good had a hole through his thigh and Sir Henry had a deep cut along his jaw line.

Luckily, Good was a decent surgeon and he stitched up both the wounds.

Once we were cleaned up, we had some broth and tried to sleep. The wailing sounds of the injured rang through the night. At around midnight, only Gagool's wailing over the dead King Twala could be heard.

On the next morning, Good had a high fever and was spitting blood due to an internal injury. Even though Sir Henry seemed fresh, he could barely move. Infadoos came to meet us and he greeted Sir Henry with reverence. The Kukuana now looked upon him as a supernatural being for slaying Twala with the final "Incubu's blow".

We were told by Infadoos that Twala had decided to surrender to Ignosi as Scragga was dead and there was no rivalry for the throne.

Afterwards, Ignosi arrived, wearing a single diamond on his forehead.

"Hail, O King!" I said, rising to greet him.

"Yes, Macumazahn. I am a king at last, with your help," was his reply. He had decided to hold a great feast in two weeks to show himself to the people.

"What about Gagool?" I asked.

"She is the evil genius of the land," Ignosi answered. "I shall kill her and all the witch doctors! She has lived so long that no one remembers how old she is and she has made the land wicked."

"Yet she has a lot of knowledge, which will be destroyed if she is killed," I replied.

"That is so," he said thoughtfully. "She knows the secret of the 'Three Witches'."

"Do not forget your promise, Ignosi. You must lead us to the mines."

"I will not forget, Macumazahn," Ignosi assured me and left.

I saw that Good was delirious with fever and his condition was rapidly worsening. For the next four to five days, his condition remained critical. In fact, I was sure that he would not survive. But Foulata tended to him throughout the day and all night long, showing no sign of being tired.

On the fifth night, I saw Good lying perfectly still. I thought that the end had finally come. Going closer, I saw that he was sleeping soundly, tightly clasping Foulata's hand.

Foulata did not move for the next eighteen hours. She knelt by Good's side and held his hand as she took brief naps. She was scared that if she moved her hand, Good would wake up!

After a few days, when Good had recovered almost completely, Sir Henry told him about Foulata's untiring nursing. Upon hearing this, the sailor's eyes filled with tears. Good went straight up to her, taking me along to interpret.

"Tell her," said Good," that I owe her my life. And that I will never forget her kindness to my dying day."

I interpreted and Foulata blushed and answered, "No, my lord forgets that it was he who saved my life. I'm his servant."

A few days later, the council formally recognised Ignosi as the king.

True to his promise, Ignosi thanked the Greys and presented each man with cattle along with promotions. He issued an order that till the time we remained in Kukuanaland, we were to be treated as kings. He also proclaimed that henceforth, no man would be punished without a trial and that witch hunting was banned.

When the ceremony was over, we went with Ignosi to his hut. He said to us, "My friends, the mines are where the 'Silent Ones' sit. There is a great cave deep in the mountain, where the kings of the land are buried. There is also a deep pit that contains a secret chamber. Perhaps in there lie the stones you seek.

There is a legend in the land that many generations ago, a white man had crossed the mountains and was led by a woman to the secret chamber. He was shown the wealth hidden in the chamber. But before he could take it out, the woman betrayed him and he was driven back to the mountains. Since then, no man has entered the place.

If you find the secret chamber, you shall have these stones. As far as we know, the secret chamber was known only to Twala and Gagool. Twala is dead. Now only Gagool can lead you there."

"And if she refuses?" I asked him.

"Then she must die," said Ignosi sternly. He ordered Gagool to be brought before him. She arrived, escorted along by two guards.

"Leave her," commanded Ignosi.

Without support, Gagool dropped to the floor like a withered bundle. She asked, "What do you want, Ignosi? You dare not touch me for my magic will kill you."

"Your magic could not save Twala," replied Ignosi. "I want you to show us the chamber where the shining stones are."

"No," she protested. "I alone know the secret and I will never tell you. The white devils shall go empty-handed."

"You shall tell me or you will die."

"You will not dare to touch me! I have survived your father and his father and even his father,"

shrieked Gagool, rising up and falling back onto the floor. "I can only be killed by chance. Anyone who dares to kill me will be cursed forever."

"I will still kill you," said Ignosi, angrily seizing his spear. He got up and put his spear at her throat. "Will you show me where the stones are or do you wish to die?"

With a wild yell, Gagool jumped up and then fell on the floor once again.

"I will show you. I only ask that you let me live," said Gagool.

"Tomorrow, you shall go with Infadoos and my white brothers to the place. And if you betray them, I will kill you slowly."

"I will not betray you, Ignosi. But remember, once before, it was a woman who showed the chamber to a white man and evil befell him," she said.

Her wicked eyes glinted and she laughed evilly as she promised to lead the way.

## Chapter Sixteen

# The Place of Death

That very day, along with Good, Sir Henry, Foulata, Infadoos, Gagool and a few of the natives, I set out for the "Three Witches" mountains. One of the natives pointed the path to us and hurriedly waved goodbye to us.

Gagool grumbled and muttered and cursed all the way, but we didn't pay much attention to her. It took us three days to reach the foot of the middle mountain.

As we treaded our way up the mountain, I wondered if we were going to meet the same fate as the old Dom and perhaps also Sir Henry's brother, George.

We went on until we came to a vast, circular hole. It was three hundred feet or more in depth and half a mile round.

"Can you guess what this is?" I asked Sir Henry and Good. They shook their heads.

"You may depend on it that this is the entrance to Solomon's diamond mines," I said.

"Look there," I said, pointing to a series of worn flat slabs of stone that were placed on a gentle slope below the level of a watercourse.

"Those tables were once used to wash the stuff," I declared.

At the other edge of the vast hole were three towering figures. As we drew near, we recognised the colossal "Silent Ones." Two male figures and one female figure were set on huge pedestals of dark rock. The female form was nude. Rising from either side of her head were the points of a crescent. The statues measured about thirty feet from the crown to the pedestal. They formed the most awe-inspiring trinity, standing in solitude and gazing across the plain forever.

Infadoos walked up to us and asked if we intended to enter the "Place of Death" at once or if we would wait till we had eaten. If we were ready to go at once, Gagool had announced her willingness to guide us.

We decided to proceed instantly, taking food and water with us in a reed basket.

Straight ahead arose a sheer wall of rock, more than eighty feet high. This wall formed the base of a lofty peak. Gagool hobbled off towards the wall. We followed her.

Soon, Gagool stopped at a narrow portal with an arch around it. She turned to look at us and announced, "White men from the Stars, great warriors Incubu and Bougwan, and Macumazahn the wise, are you ready?"

"We are ready," I said.

"Good! Make your hearts strong. Infadoos, you who betrayed your master, will you come?"

Infadoos answered with a frown, "No, but if you hurt my lords, you will die."

"I hear, Infadoos. Come on, here is the lamp" she said, hobbling forward.

"Are you coming, Foulata?" asked Good. Though the young girl was scared, she would not leave Good's side, so she nodded bravely.

We followed Gagool into the passage. As we walked in, we realised that there was light ahead. In another minute, we were in the most wonderful place we had ever seen.

We were in the hall of the vastest cathedral. It was lit and ventilated by shafts opening outside from the roof, arched a hundred feet above our heads.

But its stupendous size was the least of the wonders, for there stood gigantic pillars of huge stalactites in rows. Some of these were about twenty feet in diameter at the base and rose with delicate beauty to the distant roof. On one of these pillars, we discovered the figure of an ancient Egyptian god.

From the main aisle opened smaller caves. We could not linger here as Gagool had hastened on. She led us straight to the top of the vast and silent cave, where we found another doorway, similar to the one found in Egyptian temples.

"Are you prepared to enter the Place of Death, white men?" asked Gagool.

"Lead on," Good said solemnly.

Gagool trotted along, chuckling hideously. I reluctantly followed and found myself in a gloomy, poorly lit cave that was forty feet long and thirty feet high.

At first, all I could see was a massive stone table on the other side. Then I spotted a fifteen-foot high figure. It was a giant skeleton of Death himself. It was a great white skeleton that rose high above us, looking scary. In its bony fingers, it held a great white spear that was aimed at anyone who stood before it.

We stopped for a moment to gaze at the mighty skeleton before us. It was a sight to behold.

After a while, we looked around. I noticed Gagool furtively glancing at something across the room, so I followed her gaze.

Next, I discovered a brown thing, seated in one corner. A minute later, my eyes grew accustomed to the light and I saw what that thing was.

"Great heavens!" I said feeling faint.

I tried to walk out that very minute, but Sir Henry caught me by my collar and held me back.

"What is that?" Wondered Sir Henry, pointing to the brown thing seated on the table. But the minute he got a good look, he let go of me. As for Good, he swore feebly, while Foulata threw her arms round his neck and shrieked. Only Gagool chuckled loudly. It was an awful sight.

"Hee! Hee! Hee!" Laughed Gagool. "Come, Incubu, you who are so brave in battle. Come and see him for yourself."

Sir Henry stared stupefied. The brown figure was the same man he had defeated just a few days ago — Twala himself!

A thin glassy film had gathered over the surface of Twala's corpse. We observed that water fell steadily on the corpse's neck from the roof of the chamber. From there, it ran down over the entire surface, and finally escaped into the rock.

We stared at the sight in front of us. Twala's body was being transformed into a stalactite!

A look at the other white forms seated on the stone bench confirmed this. They were human bodies indeed, but now they were stalactites. This was the way in which the Kukuana people had, from time immemorial, preserved their royal dead–by turning them into stalactites!

It was an awe-inspiring sight.

## Chapter Seventeen

# Solomon's Treasure Chamber

Upon our insistence, Gagool led us further towards the secret chamber. Once there, she placed a gourd of oil on the floor and said, "My lords, light your lamps."

I did as I was told and lit a torch but saw nothing except solid rock. "Do not fool us," I said sternly.

"I do not, my lord. See for yourself!" She said, pointing to the solid rock. I held up the torch and saw the gigantic mass of stone rising slowly from the floor and vanishing into the rock above. The rock must have weighed at least thirty tonnes. Very slowly, the great stone moved itself till it vanished altogether and a dark hole lay open before us. It was a mystery how the massive stone was set in motion. I was sure that there was some simple lever which was moved by applying some pressure to a secret spot.

"Enter, white men from the Stars," said Gagool, talking to me and the group who stood just behind. "But, listen to what I have to say. The bright stones you will see inside were dug out from the pit over which the 'Silent Ones' sit. This place has been entered only once since the stones were brought here. It was a white man and a native woman who discovered the secret of this stone door by chance. You would not have found it in a million years.

The white man started filling the stones in a goat skin bag. Then, as he was leaving the chamber, he took one more large stone."

"What happened to Da Silvestre?" I asked.

"How do you know the dead man's name?" Gagool asked sharply. But she went on.

"No one knows what happened to him. We only know that the white man was frightened, for he flung down the goat skin bag filled with the stones and fled out with just one stone. That is the stone that the kings wore in their diadem and it is the same stone that King Ignosi now wears."

"Has no one entered here since then?" I asked.

"No one, my lords. The secret of the door is passed on to every king. Many kings have opened the door but never entered. But enter, my lords. If I speak the truth, you will find the goat-skin bag with the stones in it. And if there is evil, you will learn about it afterwards," she said.

Gagool hobbled down the passage, taking the lighted oil gourd. All the others followed, including Foulata, who was very frightened. I hesitated, but soon followed.

We reached an entrance. "See, my lords," said Gagool, holding the light before her. "Those who stored the treasure here fled in haste," pointing towards the unfinished work of placing stone blocks along the passage. Scared, Foulata refused

187

to go further and decided to wait at the inner entrance of the chamber.

We went further till we saw an elaborately painted wooden door. Across its threshold lay a goat-skin bag.

"Hee! Hee! White men," sniggered Gagool. "See, I told you, the white man who came here fled in haste and dropped the bag. Look inside!"

Good picked up the heavy bag. "By Jove! It's full of diamonds," he whispered, awed.

Sir Henry took the lamp from Gagool's hand and we entered through the doorway into King Solomon's treasure chamber.

The room was about ten square feet large. We saw a splendid collection of elephant tusks stored on one of the arches of the roof. On the opposite side of the chamber were about a score of large wooden boxes that were painted red.

"There are the diamonds," I cried, opening the top box. Sir Henry held the light over the box and we saw strange-shaped gold pieces inside.

"At least, we will not go back empty-handed," I said, awe-struck.

"But," said Good, "I don't see diamonds."

"My lords! Look where it is darkest to find the stones," said Gagool. "There are three stone chests there, two are sealed and one is open."

We went to the corner that Gagool had pointed. We saw that the open chest was three-parts full of large, uncut diamonds. Stooping, I picked some up. "We are the richest men in the whole world," I said.

"Hee! Hee!" Cackled Gagool. "Now you have the bright stones you love, white men. Take them, eat them and drink them."

We burst out laughing at her ridiculous suggestion. When we opened the other chests, they too were filled with diamonds to the brim.

We did not notice Gagool stealthily slipping out of the treasure room. All of a sudden, we heard Foulata cry, "Help! The stone falls! Help! Help! She has stabbed me!"

We ran down the passage. To our horror, we saw the rock coming down slowly. It was only three feet above the floor. Near the stone struggled Foulata and Gagool. Foulata was holding on to the old witch.

Suddenly, Gagool broke free and crawled beneath the heavy stone, but it was too late! There was not enough space for her to crawl through. Gagool shrieked in agony and, in a long sickening crunch, the stone crushed her completely.

Turning around, we saw that Foulata was stabbed and would not survive. "Ah! Bougwan, I shall die!" Gasped Foulata.

"Poor girl!" Good cried in distress and began kissing her.

"Bougwan," she said, after a pause," is Macumazahn there?"

"Here I am, Foulata," I went up to her.

"Macumazahn, please tell Bougwan that I love him. And that I am glad to die because I know that I cannot be with him," as she spoke these last words, she died.

"She is dead!" Sobbed Good, tears running down his face as he held onto her.

"Don't fret, old fellow," said Sir Henry, "we will soon join her, as we shall be buried alive."

It was then that we realised the horror of our situation. The stone door was closed and the only person who knew how to open it was dead. Now, it could only be blasted open with large quantities of dynamite, which we didn't have.

We realised how cleverly Gagool had trapped us. What a horrible, slow end we would have, perishing of thirst and hunger, surrounded by King Solomon's treasure! Now I understood her sneer about drinking and eating diamonds.

"We need to find the spring that opens the stone door before the lamp goes out," said Sir Henry. Spurred into action, we began to feel up and down the sides of the passage. But there was no knob or spring to discover.

"I think," I said, "that it does not work from the inside. If it did, Gagool would not have risked trying to crawl underneath the stone."

Sir Henry said, "There is nothing we can do about the door. Let us go back to the treasure room." With a heavy heart, we returned to the room, taking the food basket and Foulata's corpse with us. We then divided the food and water amongst ourselves to make it last longer. The torch began to dim.

"Quatermain," said Sir Henry, "what's the time?"

"It's 6 pm. We had entered at 11 am." A thought struck me. I said, "Surely, Infadoos will look for us if we don't return tonight?"

Sir Henry replied, "He will search in vain as he does not know the secret of the stone door. Only Gagool knew it. My friends, the search for treasure has brought many to a bad end. Now we shall join their ranks."

The torch emitted its light for one last time. Then the flame sank and died. We sat there in the cold, dark cave, shivering and waiting to meet our fate.

# Chapter Eighteen

# We Abandon Hope

We were in an ironical situation. Unimaginable treasure lay all around us and yet we would give it all away for the faintest chance of escape.

"Good," Sir Henry said at last, "how many matches do you have left?"

"Eight, Curtis."

"Strike one and let us see the time."

He did so and the flare blinded us. It was 5 am by my watch.

"We had better eat something," I suggested. So we all ate a little and drank some water.

Sir Henry suggested that we should crawl near the door and shout in the hope that someone

would hear our voice. Accordingly, Good yelled loudly at the door for a time. But his yells had no effect. At 7 am, an idea occurred to me. "How is it," said I, "that we have fresh air here? Where is it coming from?"

Good said, "I never thought of that. It can't come through the air-tight stone door."

The three of us started examining the ground on our hands and knees, feeling for a draught. After we had looked for over an hour or more, Sir Henry and I gave up in despair. But Good continued to search.

Suddenly, he shouted, "Come here!" We went to him. "Quatermain, put your hand where mine is. Do you feel anything?"

"I think I feel air coming up."

"Now listen." He rose and stamped upon the place. It rang hollow. With trembling hands, he lit a match and we saw that we were in the far corner of the chamber. There was a joint in the solid rock floor and there, in level with the rock, was a stone ring.

We were excited. Good scratched around the ring with his knife. Finally, he worked his knife under the ring to keep the hook intact. The ring began to move. When it was upright, he thrust his hands into it and tugged at it with all his force, but nothing budged. Both Sir Henry and I tried but failed.

Good again scratched all around the crack where we had felt the air coming up.

"Now, Curtis," he said, "put your back into it. Quatermain, Curtis, grip around the griddle and pull when I say the word."

Sir Henry put in all his enormous strength and I did the same. Suddenly there was a grating sound, then a rush of air and we were all on our backs with a heavy flag-stone on top of us.

"Light a match, Good," said Curtis. He did so, and there before us was a stone staircase. We started to go down the stairs, carrying the remaining food and water with us.

As we were leaving the chamber, it occurred to me that we had not thought about the diamonds in the last twenty-four hours. I decided to take a few, in case we got out of this place alive. I filled my pockets with them. I also stuffed Foulata's basket and the water gourds with great quantities of diamonds.

"Come on, Quatermain," called Sir Henry. We descended the stairs. At the end of it, we lit another match and saw that we were now standing in the middle of a narrow tunnel.

Of course, it was impossible to know where the tunnel went and we were not too sure if we should go left or right. Suddenly, it occurred to Good that when I had lit the match, the draught of the passage had blown the flame to the left.

"Let us go against the draught," he said. "Air draws inwards, not outwards."

We moved slowly and carefully, holding onto the walls in order to stick to the path. We walked through what seemed a dark labyrinth. Finally, after walking for quite a few hours, we decided to stop and eat something.

We were exhausted and depressed. Just as we finished eating, I thought that I heard a sound. It was faint and far away.

"It's running water," said Good suddenly. We started again in the direction of the faint murmur. As we went further, the sound of rushing water became more audible.

"Go gently, Good," warned Sir Henry. "We seem to be close."

Just as he said this, we heard a loud splash. Good had fallen into the water.

"Good! Where are you?" We shouted, terrified. To our intense relief, an answer came back in a choky voice.

"I am all right! I've got hold of a rock. Strike a light to show me where you are."

Hastily, I lit the last remaining match. We saw that a dark mass of water was running at our feet. A few feet away, Good was hanging on to a projecting rock for dear life. His face looked as pale as a ghost.

"Stand clear to catch me," called out Good. "I have no choice but to swim for it."

He let go off the rock and slowly swam towards us. Our hands were stretched out eagerly to grab a hold of him as soon as he came close. Finally, he grabbed Sir Henry's outstretched hand and we pulled him out of the water.

"My word!" He said, between gasps, "If I hadn't managed to catch that rock, I would have been done. I could feel no bottom!"

After Good had rested for a while, we began to retrace our steps along the tunnel. Soon, we came to another gallery leading to our right.

"We may as well take it," said Sir Henry wearily. For a long while we stumbled along the path, utterly exhausted.

Suddenly, Sir Henry stopped and we bumped against him. "Look!" He whispered, "are my eyes playing a trick on me or do I see light?"

We stared ahead with our eyes bulging out. Just then, we saw a faint, glimmering spot of light. With a gasp of hope we pushed on.

Soon enough, we felt a faint breeze roll around us. It felt like hope. I was now starting to think that we would escape after all.

But as we went further, the tunnel narrowed and, soon, it was as small as a fox hole. We had to squeeze through it with great difficulty. After an eternity, we tumbled out, rolling over grass, through bushes and soft, wet soil.

We just sat down together, overwhelmed to have escaped from the awful dungeon which could have become our grave.

Presently, in the light of dawn, we saw each other's gaunt-cheeked, hollow-eyed, bruised, bleeding, dust-smeared bodies. We were a frightful sight. And yet, Good's eye-glass was fixed in place!

We were at the bottom of the vast pit. We started climbing up slowly and painfully. At last, we stood on a great road by the side of the pit, opposite to the Colossi.

# Chapter Nineteen

# Ignosi's Farewell

We saw some huts by the side of the road and staggered towards them. Suddenly, one of the figures rose. It was Infadoos.

"Oh, my lords, you have come back from the dead!" The old warrior wept for joy.

In the days that followed, Good mourned Foulata's death. I mourned the loss of diamonds, for though I had taken enough to last a lifetime, I rued that some had fallen during our fall.

Before starting for Loo, we decided to go back to the stalactite caves and find the spring that would open the stone door. We could not find it. At last, we gave up and started for Loo.

Ten days later we were cordially received by Ignosi. He listened with interest to our wonderful story but on hearing about Gagool's frightful end, he became thoughtful.

"Come here," he called to a very old councillor. "Tell me all that you know about Gagool, the witch doctress. How was she before she turned into a witch doctor? Was she young, like you?"

"No, my King! She was old and dried even in my great grandfather's time, as old as she is now. She has always been full of wickedness."

"She is no more," revealed Ignosi.

"O King! An ancient curse has been taken away from the land," said the councillor.

"You see, my brothers," said Ignosi, turning to us, "Gagool was a strange woman and I am happy that she is dead. She would have let you die in the dark place. Perhaps she would have killed me as she killed my father. But go on with the tale. Surely there never was a tale like it!"

I narrated the full story of our escape to Ignosi, who listened intently.

When I had finished, I told Ignosi about our desire to depart from Kukuanaland.

"Ignosi," I said, "the time has come for us to return to our own land. You came with us as a servant and now we leave you as a mighty king. If you are grateful to us, remember to rule justly and to respect the law so that you prosper. Tomorrow, at day break, will you give us an escort to lead us across the mountains?"

Ignosi covered his face with his hands for a while before answering.

"My heart is sore," he said at last. "What have I done to you, O Incubu, Macumazahn and Bougwan, that you want to leave me? You who stood by me in rebellion and in battle, will you leave me during my days of peace and victory? What can I give you to make you stay here?"

"Ignosi, we seek our world," I answered.

"Do you love the bright stones more than you love your friend?" asked Ignosi bitterly, his eyes flashing with hurt and anger.

I laid my hand upon his arm. "Ignosi," I told him, "tell us, when YOU wandered in Zululand and among the white people, did your heart not yearn for your father's land?"

"Yes, Macumazahn," he spoke, his face reflecting his pain and sadness.

"In the same way, Ignosi, our hearts yearn for our land."

There was a silence. When Ignosi broke it, his voice told us that he finally understood.

"I see that now, as always, your words are wise and full of reason, Macumazahn. If you wish to go, I will not stop you. I know that I will never hear from you again. But listen to me. From now on, no other white man shall cross the mountains to seek the shining stones. I should see no traders with their guns. If someone comes, I will send a regiment to fill up the pit and break down the white columns in the caves so that no one can reach that door that you spoke of.

However, for the three of you, who are very dear to me, there is always a place for you here.

Infadoos, my uncle, shall take you across the mountains. There is another way to cross them. Farewell, my brothers, my brave white friends. I will make a decree and it shall be spread far and wide. Your names — Incubu, Macumazahn and Bougwan — shall be 'hlonipa' or sacred and he who speaks them without respect shall die.

Your memory shall be preserved in the land forever. Always prosper, Incubu, Macumazahn, and Bougwan, my lords and my friends."

Ignosi rose and looked earnestly at us for a few seconds. Then he threw the corner of his karross over his head and covered his face.

We went out in silence.

On the next day, at dawn, we left Loo. Leading our company was our old friend Infadoos, who was heart-broken at our departure.

As we walked out of the kraal, the natives stepped out of their houses. Soon, all the main streets of the kraal were lined with multitudes of people. They gave us the royal salute as we passed by.

Suddenly, a pretty young girl ran to Good and said that she had a boon to ask. "Ask" he said, wondering what her request would be.

"My lord, please show us your white legs for one last time so that we can tell our grandchildren about them. I have travelled for four days just to see them."

Sir Henry and I looked away, trying very hard not to laugh. Good blushed with embarrassment, he refused to do any such thing.

"Come, my dear fellow," said Sir Henry. "You can't refuse to oblige a lady."

"I won't," replied Good, obstinately.

However, he relented and kept his trousers drawn up to his knees until we left Loo.

Four days later, Infadoos had taken us to a place where it was possible to climb down the wall of the cliff that separated Kukuanaland from the desert. The path was accidentally discovered by some ostrich hunters. They had also discovered an oasis in the desert.

We were to begin our climb down the precipice. We bid farewell to the sturdy, old Infadoos. He solemnly wished us good bye.

"Never, my lords," he said," shall my old eyes see you again." Good was so moved that he gifted his spare eye-glass to Infadoos, who was delighted and said that it would greatly increase his prestige. After several attempts, he managed to wear it in his eye.

We started climbing down and reached the bottom in the evening, which is when we decided to stop and rest for the night.

"Do you know," said Sir Henry, "I think that there are worse places than Kukuanaland in the world? I have known unhappier times before, but never such strange ones."

"I almost wish I were back," sighed Good.

As for myself, I thought that we were lucky to be alive.

On the next morning, we started our trudge across the desert. We had a good supply of water that was carried by our five guides. By noon of

the third day's journey, we could see the trees of an oasis.

The strangest thing happened once we reached the oasis. We found a hut under the shade of a fig tree, in the middle of nowhere.

"What the dickens," I said to myself, "can a hut be doing here, in the middle of nowhere?"

## Chapter Twenty

# Found

We neared the hut and stood outside, staring at it curiously. It was obvious that someone lived here, in the middle of nowhere.

"It is impossible!" I thought. "No hunter would ever come here, leave aside settle down here." As we stared at each other, Sir Henry and Good came up to me.

Just then, we spotted a man coming out of the hut. He was clearly a white man, but he was dressed in animal skins and he had an enormous beard. I turned to look at Good and Sir Henry.

"Is that a white man or am I mad?" I asked them. The man began to limp towards us.

As Good and Sir Henry looked on, the lame white man uttered a great cry and began hobbling towards us. When he was close, he fell down. With a spring Sir Henry was by his side. "Great Powers!" He cried. "It is my brother, George!"

Another figure, also clad in skins, emerged from the hut. He was holding a gun in his hand. When he saw Sir Henry's brother lying on the ground, he ran towards us.

On seeing me, he stopped in his tracks and suddenly shouted in delight, "Macumazahn! Is that really you?"

I nodded, not quite recognising the man who stood before me.

"I'm Jim the hunter!" He said. "Do you remember the note you gave me to pass on to Bass? I lost that note and we have been living in this oasis for nearly two years."

The man fell at my feet and wept for joy. I lifted him by the arms and gave him a brief hug, happy to see him. I had never thought that I would see him again.

Meanwhile, Sir Henry and his brother continued to look at each other, their past quarrels forgotten. Sir Henry had finally found what he had come looking for and just when he had almost given up!

"My dear old fellow," burst out Sir Henry at last, "I thought you were dead. All of us went looking for you all the way to Solomon's Mountains! I had given up all hope of ever seeing you again and now, here I come across you, living in the desert, far away from everyone."

George Curtis smiled tearfully at his brother. I walked up to him and waved lightly.

"How do you do, Mr Neville?" I asked him. "Do you remember me?"

"Why," he said, "if it isn't Hunter Quatermain, eh!" He shook my hand happily and looked at Good, who was smiling widely at him. "And Good too! My, my, this is all so very strange."

We had a quick reunion; everyone was just so happy to have found each other at last! We settled down and began discussing our adventures.

That evening, in the hut, George Curtis told us his story. Two years ago, he had started from Sitanda's Kraal to reach Suliman's Berg. Jim had lost the note I had given him. Following the directions of the natives, they had tried to reach Solomon's Mountains, taking the path that we had just taken.

George continued, "But when we reached this oasis, a boulder fell on my leg and crushed it. After that, I was unable to go further. This oasis had ample food and water, so we have lived here. For two years now, we have been hoping that some natives might come here and help us find our way home.

Only last night, we had decided that Jim should leave me and try to reach Sitanda's Kraal to get assistance. And now, you turn up and find me where you least expected! It is the most wonderful thing to have happened."

Once he was done, Sir Henry told him about our adventures.

"By Jove!" said George at the end of our tale. I showed him some of the diamonds.

"At least you got something for your troubles, besides my worthless self," rued George.

Sir Henry laughed. "The diamonds belong to Quatermain and Good. It was a part of the bargain that they should divide any treasure they might find."

Later, I consulted with Good and told Sir Henry that a third of the diamonds belonged to him. If Sir Henry did not want them, we would give them to his brother George. Sir Henry agreed but George did not know about this till later.

We accomplished our journey across the desert with difficulty as we had to support George.

When we reached Sitanda's Kraal six months later, we found that our guns and belongings were safe. Finally, we reached, Berea, near Durban, where I am now writing. I bid farewell to all who accompanied me through the strangest trip I have ever made.

At this point, I think that I shall end my history.

P.S. Just as I had written the last word, a servant came carrying a letter. It is from Sir Henry and it reads as follows.

*October 1, 1884.*

*Brayley Hall,*

*Yorkshire.*

*My dear Quatermain,*

*I send you a line to say that the three of us, George, Good and myself, made it to England. You should have seen what a handsome devil Good turned into the very next day, beautifully shaved, wearing a frock coat, brand new eye-glass, etc., etc.*

*To come to business, Good and I took the diamonds to Streeter's to be valued, as we arranged. I am afraid to tell you what they put them at, it seems so enormous! It appears that, with the exception of one or two of the largest, they are of the finest water and equal in every way to the best Brazilian stones. I asked them if they would buy them but they said that it was beyond their power to do so. They recommended us to sell them by degrees, over a period of years. However,*

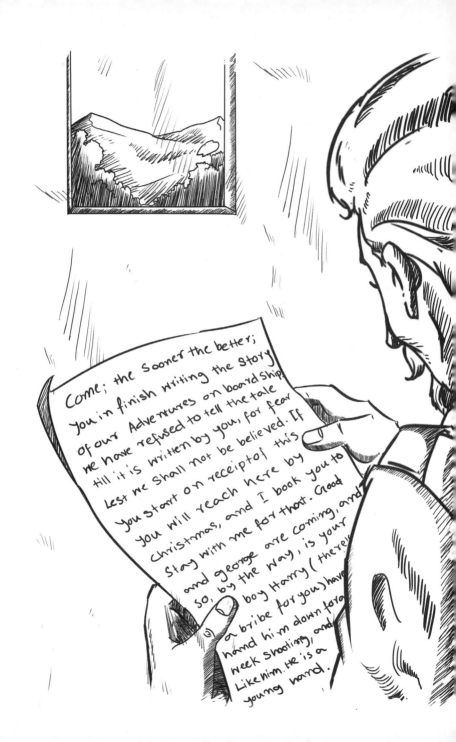

they offer a hundred and eighty thousand for a very small portion of them.

You must come home, Quatermain, and see these things, especially if you insist upon making the magnificent present of the third share, which does not belong to me nor to my brother George.

As for Good, he is no good. I think he is still pining over Foulata. He told me that he hadn"t seen another woman, even after returning home.

I want you to come home, my dear old comrade, and to buy a house near here. You have done your day's work and have lots of money now. There is a place for sale quite close by, which would suit you admirably. Do come. The sooner, the better.

You can finish writing the story of our adventures aboard the ship. We have refused to tell the tale until it is written by you. If you start upon the receipt of this letter, you will reach here by Christmas. Good is coming and George; and by the way, so is your boy Harry. (There's a bribe for you).

Goodbye, old man; I can't say anymore, but I know that you will come.

*Your sincere friend,*
*Henry Curtis.*

*P.S: The tusks of the great bull that killed poor Khiva have been put up in the hall here, over the pair of buffalo horns you gave me. They look magnificent. The axe with which I killed Twala is fixed above my writing-table. I wish that we could have managed to bring away the coats of chain armour. Don't lose poor Foulata's basket in which you brought the diamonds.*

*H.C.*

Today is Tuesday. There is a steamer going on Friday and I think that I must take Curtis at his word and sail by her for England. Perhaps it is only to see you, Harry, my boy and to look after the printing of this history, which is a task that I do not like to trust anybody else with.

About the Author

# ■ Sir Henry Rider Haggard

Sir Henry Rider Haggard was an English writer of adventure novels set in exotic locations, predominantly Africa. One of the best-selling novelists of the nineteenth century, his stories continue to be popular and influential to this day and age.

*King Solomon's Mines* was Haggard's breakout novel. Written in six weeks on a bet, Haggard had almost sold the manuscript to a publisher for a paltry 500 pounds. At the last minute, he insisted on 10% of the royalties, which set him up for life.

*King Solomon's Mines* is considered the first of the Lost World genre and has inspired dozens of adventure stories, including Edgar Rice Burroughs's Tarzan books and the Indiana Jones movies.

Haggard wrote over 50 novels. He was made a Knight Bachelor in 1912 and a Knight Commander of the Order of the British Empire in 1919. The locality of Rider, British Columbia, was named in his memory.

# ■ Characters

**Allan Quatermain** - The narrator of the novel, he is an elephant hunter. Quatermain plays upon the superstitious nature of the Kukuanas to his own advantage. He claims to be a coward, but his actions demonstrate his bravery.

**Sir Henry Curtis** - He desires to find his brother George. Sir Henry proves, time and again, to be a man of great bravery and heroism. He is also compassionate and often comforts the despairing Quatermain and Good during their misfortunes.

**Captain John Good** - A retired naval officer, Good is fastidious about his personal appearance. His extreme focus on his dress gives the men a means of convincing the Kukuanas that they are supernatural beings. Good always wears an eye-glass.

**George Neville** - George, Sir Henry Curtis' brother, changes his name to Neville in Africa. He gets lost while hunting for King Solomon's mines.

**José Silvestre** - José Silvestre was a Portuguese explorer. While dying, he gave Quatermain a map that showed the location of King Solomon's mines.

**Ventvogel** - A member of the Hottentot tribe, he is hired by Quatermain for the safari.

**Umbopa** - Hired as a servant for the expedition, he turns out to be Ignosi, son of the rightful king of the Kukuanas. Ignosi is dignified, of noble bearing and loyal to his friends.

**Khiva** - Khiva is a brave and loyal Zulu hired by Quatermain.

**Infadoos** - Infadoos is a native sub-chieftain among the Kukuanas. He helps Ignosi regain kingship of the tribe.

**Twala** - Twala is a hideous one-eyed king of the Kukuana land. He is a cruel king who came by his throne through guile and murder. Twala is cunning and brave.

**Gagool** - Gagool is a native sorceress. She is generations old and maintains her power through the agency of witch-finders.

**Foulata** - Foulata is a beautiful Kukuana maiden who develops a strong affection for Captain Good.

**Scragga** - Scragga is Twala's cruel son.

# ■ Questions

## Chapter 1

- *Where did Quatermain first meet Sir Henry and Captain Good?*
- *Why had Sir Henry and Captain Good travelled to Africa?*

## Chapter 2

- *Who told Quatermain first about King Solomon's Mines?*
- *What did the dying man give Quatermain?*

## Chapter 3

- *What were the terms and conditions put forth by Quatermain to join Sir Henry?*
- *Describe the last servant hired by Quatermain for the expedition.*

## Chapter 4

- *What happened to the elephant that Good had shot?*
- *How did Khiva die?*

## Chapter 5

- *What did the men carry in their travel kit?*
- *What did the adventurers do to protect themselves from the hot sun?*

## Chapter 6

- *How did Ventvogel detect the presence of water?*
- *What did Umbopa find on top of the lava plateau?*

## Chapter 7
- *Describe Solomon's Great Road.*
- *Why did the natives feel afraid of the white men?*

## Chapter 8
- *Who was Infadoos? How was he related to king Twala?*
- *What kind of a person was Scragga?*

## Chapter 9
- *Why did Sir Henry get angry with Twala on the first day of the annual feast?*
- *How did Quatermain make the natives believe that they had supernatural powers?*

## Chapter 10
- *What did Umbopa show the chiefs to prove that he was King Imotu's son?*
- *Which men did Gagool target during the witch hunt?*

## Chapter 11
- *What additional sign did Quatermain give to convince the chiefs that Ignosi was the rightful king?*
- *Why was Foulata chosen for the sacrifice?*

## Chapter 12
- *Where did Quatermain and the others go after blackening out the moon?*
- *What were Twala's terms for surrendering before the battle?*

**Chapter 13**

- *Why did Ignosi decide to initiate the attack on Twala's army?*
- *When did Quatermain join the fray?*

**Chapter 14**

- *Why did Twala seek out Sir Henry to attack?*
- *Where did the defeated army of Twala take refuge?*

**Chapter 15**

- *Who nursed Good back to health? How?*
- *How did Ignosi convince Gagool to lead the white men to the Mines?*

**Chapter 16**

- *Who are the "Silent Ones"?*
- *What is the "Place of Death"?*

**Chapter 17**

- *What did the men see inside King Solomon's treasure room?*
- *Why did Gagool ask the men to eat and drink the bright stones?*

**Chapter 18**

- *What was the first hope for the men that they could escape the treasure room?*
- *What did Quatermain carry in the reed basket?*

## Chapter 19

- *Why did Quatermain want to leave Kukuanaland?*
- *What arrangements did Ignosi make to help the men out of the Kukuanaland?*

## Chapter 20

- *Why was Neville living in the oasis?*
- *What was Neville's reaction on seeing Sir Henry?*